Priscilla Alone

Alone Trilogy
Book 1

Judith Bixby-Boling

ISBN: 978-1-7358687-0-7

For Mary Benton

Prologue

October 1865
Riverbend Farm
Near Norwich, Connecticut

I sat in my favorite chair, sewing the dress I planned to wear to the church social Saturday next. A shiver coursed through my person, and I pulled the shawl closer around my shoulders. Susanna had been late laying the fire in the family parlor, and the night's chill lingered.

Thoughts of Ethan Brandt crowded my thoughts. We planned to be wed when he mustered out of the Connecticut Volunteers. But a Confederate Soldier shot and killed him at the Battle of Averasboro in North Carolina on 16 March of this year.

A tear escaped my eye, and I brushed it away with my fingertips before it splashed on the dress in my lap.

Papa had retired to his study after supper but now opened the parlor door and slipped into the room. Taking the winged chair next to the fireplace, he leaned close to the hearth and rubbed his hands together. His demeanor was disquieting, and I sensed something weighed heavily on his mind.

"Priscilla," he uttered softly as he stared into the flames.

"Papa, is there something you wish to speak with me about?"

He did not immediately respond but finally said, "Yes. I don't know how to say it." His gaze remained focused on the fire.

"You have always told me to begin at the beginning."

"I don't know where that would be," he murmured.

"What is it? Is there more trouble?" Trepidation threatened my composure.

"I have made some decisions that will profoundly affect both of us." He closed his eyes tightly, wrinkled his nose, and compressed his lips, conveying the impression of physical pain. He grew pale, visible even in the firelight. His hands trembled.

"Are you ill? Should I have Duncan summon Doctor Jamison?"

"No, I'm not ill. Stuart Jamison can do nothing for me."

"Then, please, do not keep me in suspense. What is troubling you?"

With a sigh that I feared would remove all the air from his body, he said, "There are American Colonization Society ships leaving for Africa in six months' time. I shall be on one of those ships." He slumped in his chair, now looking at the floor.

The needle fell from my fingers as I worked to understand his meaning. Father had never been overtly political. Although I had been taught never to question his decisions, I heard myself utter the word I was thinking, "Why?"

"Because I say that I abhor the treatment of the Negros, but do nothing about it. I do not employ a single one. I did not fight in that accursed war. In fact, I paid three hundred dollars to avoid going. God help me. I paid to keep Jeremiah and Fenwick on the farm, as well. The Society ships will be carrying a thousand Negros. I mean to help those poor souls settle in Liberia."

"You supplied the Connecticut Volunteers with horses, grain, and hay from our fields. You provided the funds to purchase fabric and thread for me to sew shirts and quilts and wool to knit socks for the Sanitary. Papa, we did our part."

"No, I did not, Priscilla." He leaned forward, his face in his hands, as though defeated. "I profited handsomely from the sale of the horses and the grain and hay. Many times over the cost of the cloth and thread you used so well. I made business decisions during the war that were quite lucrative.

"I wish I could say the wealth I've accumulated was earned by the sweat of my brow, but that would be a lie. I unwittingly earned much of it in a less than honorable manner." He stared vacantly at the portrait of my mother that hung on the wall above my head. "Now I'm paying the price for that greed."

I tried to keep my face impassive as I looked at my father and took in what he told me. I prayed I was not to travel with him. Water conveyances frightened me.

We sat in silence for several minutes, neither of us knowing what to say.

"I shan't be returning. I shall live out my days in Africa. I've started liquidating my assets. I'm selling Riverbend to Samuel Martin. He's wanted the northern forty acres for many years. Catherine has been taking in orphans, and they're living atop one another. They will move into this house. It will be in good hands."

I was astounded. "Where am I to go?" I whispered. "Will I go to live in Norwich with Aunt Marian?"

Father looked at me for the first time since he entered the room. The pain of what he was telling me was writ on his face. He seemed to have aged ten years in a span of minutes.

"No, you will not go to live with your godmother," he announced, straightening his back and cheering almost too much. "I have betrothed you to Mr. Josiah Pennyman. Circumstances will not permit him to escort you to his home. You shall travel to him." His speech was rapid, as though he had to say it before he lost his courage.

A multitude of questions crowded my mind. None of them were spoken. I stared at this man, whom I thought I knew so well but found I did not know.

"You should be pleased, Priscilla." He stood and began to pace.

I found my voice. The questions tumbled one over another. "Pleased? How can I be pleased? Am I to start a new life without you? Who is Josiah Pennyman? I don't recall being introduced to him. Where does he reside? By what means am I to travel? When do I leave? May I take Sarah...?"

He started talking before I could finish. "Stop. You do not know Mr. Pennyman. He was a business partner during the war. You will go to him in April, first by train, then by ship. The arrangements are being made.

"The house staff, including your Sarah, will be given notice. That is all you need to know." Abruptly, he left the parlor, the door shutting loudly behind him.

Papa's desire for secrecy befuddled me. I sat in the parlor long after the fire was reduced to ashes, puzzling over this turn of events.

It was difficult to imagine another family living in this house, working this land, tending our livestock. I had never considered living elsewhere. This was my home. Our home. The home of my father's people for more than ninety years. The seed of every crop now growing at *Riverbend* could be traced back to those first crops planted by Great-Grandfather Llewellyn.

I walked around the room, studying the portraits of my ancestors. They, all of them, looked tired and careworn. They had their portraits made that we might remember them and the foundations they had laid for us. I wondered what words of wisdom they would impart on this inauspicious occasion of the sale of their legacy. I had always imagined my portrait gracing one of these walls, a continuation of the Llewellyn legacy for my children and grandchildren.

Riverbend Farm was my home. It was in my blood and in every breath I took. In six months, I would leave this place. A piece of my heart would remain with this farm when the carriage bore me away to a new life in a new home.

I would not look back. I vowed never to return.

Part 1
The Journey

Chapter 1

April 1866
Boston Harbor
Boston, Massachusetts

My maid, Sarah, and I stepped out of the hired carriage onto the wharf in the dark of night. She spoke with the coachman before we carefully picked our way by the moonlight toward the pier where the *Emma* was docked. Neither of us trusted ourselves to speak. We were both heartbroken that Sarah would not make the journey with me. This would be the first time I traveled unescorted. Her last duty was to see me safely aboard.

The *Emma* was an ironclad cargo ship fitted with several cabins for human passengers. I was averse to traveling on the water and expressed my preference to journey by train or coach. Papa informed me that the fastest mode of transportation was by sea.

Somewhere in Boston Town, church bells chimed half past eleven as I boarded the ship. Simultaneously, the ship's bell rang seven times. Sarah watched me climb the ramp. When I gained the deck, I turned to wave at her, but she was halfway down the pier, returning to the carriage.

An ill-mannered crewman ushered me into a cabin below deck. He did nothing to mask his disdain, muttering something about bad luck having a woman aboard. He rushed away before I could shut the door.

I was confident I was the only woman aboard the ship and admonished myself to beware of crewmen making untoward advances. As I prepared to retire, anger and resentment rose toward my father and Josiah Pennyman for placing me in this untenable situation.

I had no knowledge of my destination. I knew only that I would be wed to Josiah Pennyman, a gentleman of my father's acquaintance. I did not like the idea of an arranged marriage to a man I had never met. But I knew better than to question my father or act contrary to his wishes as long as I lived under his roof.

Chapter 2

I awoke the next morning, somewhat disoriented, as people sometimes are when waking in unfamiliar surroundings. A shaft of light filtered through the small window, puddling on the bedclothes and lending a soft, warm glow to the room. It was sparsely furnished but clean, smelling faintly of lye soap. I could feel the undulation of the ship, a sure indication we were under sail. A cacophony of sounds surrounded and threatened to engulf me: The creaking wood of the ship, the ropes straining against their moorings and winches, men shouting and singing, something akin to laundry snapping in the wind, and the ringing of a bell.

Sarah had arranged for the luggage I would need during the voyage to be delivered to the cabin. Papa had permitted me to take a few pieces of furniture and furnishings my mother's family had bequeathed to me. These, along with clothing not required during the voyage, were crated and stored in the ship's hold.

Delivered to the cabin prior to my arrival, my baggage had been stacked haphazardly in a corner. I opened one of the two trunks and commenced my morning ablutions. Dressing without a lady's maid is difficult under the best of circumstances. It is quite challenging when aboard a vessel that is swaying and lurching in turn. I struggled to remain standing whilst fastening my corset. The cage crinoline was never still but bounced and swayed while I hooked the waistband. If the cabin had been larger, I most assuredly would have lost my balance when I jumped to settle my skirts. I stuck myself three times whilst affixing a broach to my dress. I lost count of the number of pins dropped in the course of dressing my hair—some never to be seen again. Taking twice as long as it should have to dress, I believed myself presentable and began thinking about breaking my fast.

It occurred to me that I did not know when or where I should receive my meals. Determined to prove myself self-sufficient, I made the decision to venture outside the cabin in search of sustenance. I settled a bonnet on my head and was pulling on gloves when there was a soft knock on my door.

I opened the door to a boy I judged to be about twelve years of age and nearly my height. He looked at me with bright green eyes.

The boy held himself in a confident manner, contrary to his physical impression. His clothes were grimy and threadbare, and he looked as though he'd been living in them for at least a fortnight. Matted blonde hair and black smudges on his face gave the appearance of a ragamuffin. "Good mornin', Miss. I am to bring you to Captain McClain." His tone was wooden, as though the little speech was well-rehearsed.

"Good morning," I replied, taken aback by the announcement. Recovering quickly, I took up my reticule, stepped into the companionway, and closed the cabin door.

We wound our way through a cargo hold toward the captain's wardroom at the opposite end of the ship. I was saved from taking the boy's filthy arm by the narrowness of the passageways. We walked single-file. My round hoop skirt became elliptical as it pressed against the walls and shipping crates, and I worried my dress might be spoiled. Presently, we arrived at a spacious but modestly decorated room.

A rugged-looking man sat at the head of a long table, barking orders at various other men. He stopped mid-sentence when he espied my companion and me, causing all eyes to turn toward us. I felt my face grow warm, and my hands became moist inside my gloves.

"Good Lord, men. Have you never seen a lady before? Stop your gaping and get along with your duties," the captain said in a voice much louder than was necessary. "Mr. Burke, be so kind as to bring the lady a cup of tea. And mind that the cup is clean."

The captain nearly upset his chair as he rose and strode toward us. "Thank you, Mr. Boleyn, for escorting Miss Llewellyn. You may go about your own business." Without waiting for additional orders, the boy ran for the door as though the floor was melting his gumshoes.

The room quickly emptied of all but the captain and me. He took my left hand, bowed deeply, and brushed his lips across the back of my glove. "Miss Llewellyn, allow me to introduce myself. I am Ian McClain, master and commander of the *Emma*. I trust you found your accommodations acceptable?" He guided me to the table and held a chair.

"I am pleased to make your acquaintance. The cabin is quite cozy, and I passed a restful night. Thank you for allowing me to take passage on your ship." I replied as I sat.

"The pleasure is mine. I am afraid some of my crew are unsettled about having a woman aboard. They have been cautioned to mind their duties and not our passenger. Sadly, I cannot guarantee they will all keep a civil tongue in their heads." A man entering the room caught the captain's eye.

"Ah," he smiled, taking up a napkin with great flourish, "and here is our morning meal."

We did not speak while the steward served us, placed the platters on the sideboard, and left the room.

The meal was modest, by any standard, comprising of fruit, bread, and cold roast chicken.

“Will we be at sea many weeks?" I asked.

"You will be at sea about one month.”

“Will we be calling at many ports?”

“Two.”

I had hoped for a more expansive answer, but he changed the subject.

"I have ordered the purser to prepare a sheltered space on the deck for your use. It will be out of bounds to most of the crew. I have selected trustworthy men to assist you and escort you wherever you need to go on the ship. They are most honorable gentlemen.”

“I find myself indebted to you for your kindness and generosity. I shall endeavor to be as self-sufficient as possible. I do not wish to be a burden to either you or your crew.”

“I can assure you that you will be no burden to anyone aboard this ship.”

Returning to the cabin after breakfast, I set about organizing my belongings. I pushed the two trunks about the cramped quarters. Hat and linen boxes were stowed under the bed. After setting my writing box and sewing basket on the small table, I selected a book from my limited collection and settled in the chair to read.

The book lay open in my lap, forgotten, as I wished for the thousandth time that Papa had told me more about the man I was to wed. I imagined myself married to an elderly cruel man who beat animals and small children for sport. He would not be impoverished, or my father should never have agreed to the match. My future husband would be close with his money and not allow sufficient funds to maintain a proper household. He would permit no entertaining, which would put off the neighbors. He, being many years my senior, would pass from this earth well before me. Isolated from society, childless, and friendless, I would grow old and bitter before my time. My dead body would be found only because the tax collector came calling.

Urgent knocking jolted me back to reality. I must have been fidgeting, for the book was face-down on the floor, and my crinoline had shifted uncomfortably beneath me. Cautiously, I opened the door a crack to reveal a middle-aged man. His once-white shirt was covered with stains and smudges from countless sources. The hem of his slops was mid-calf, with his lower legs and feet bereft of either stockings or shoes. His flush, round face was stricken with anxiety, and his brown eyes looked upon me with what appeared to be genuine concern.

"Miss, is everythin' a'right within? I heared the most peculiar noises comin' from inside, an' afeared for yer wellbein'. Yeh did na bring no critter aboard, didja? Them noises couldn'a come from a mite of a girl."

"I can assure you, there are no animals in here."

"I heared all sorts o' caterwaulin'. A body liked to think someone was bein' doused in cold water."

"Oh, I am so sorry." It was alarming to learn that such noises had escaped my person. "I allowed my mind to wander with most appalling thoughts. I am quite well. Thank you for enquiring." I looked at him with equal concern for his health.

"Vera good, vera good," he replied. His breathing and the color of his face returned to normal as a look of relief crossed his face. "I'm Bert. The Cap'n sent me to look after yeh durin' this watch. The weather is quite pleasant this mornin'. Would yeh not prefer ta take some fresh air?"

"I am pleased to make your acquaintance, Bert. I am Miss Priscilla Llewellyn."

"Pleased ta meet yeh, ta be sure," he said with a slight bow from the waist.

"Oh, Bert," I declared. "I would love to take some air on deck if it isn't too much trouble." Leaving no room for him to comment further, I opened the door wider, then retrieved the book from the floor, placed an old gray bonnet on my head, and gathered my green shawl, tan cotton gloves, and black parasol before closing the door as I stepped over the threshold. Following Bert in the opposite direction than I had been taken earlier, I tried to pay attention to our route.

I made several failed attempts to climb the ladder that would take me above deck. In frustration, I concluded that climbing a vertical ladder whilst wearing a crinoline was not a task to be mastered in mixed company. With Bert standing lookout, I eventually devised a method by which I gained the deck without anyone being able to see much more than a bit of ankle.

On deck, the sky was nearly cloudless, the sun shone bright, and a gentle breeze teased a stray tendril of my auburn hair. Deep blue ocean expanded as far as I could see.

"Oh, Bert, this is beautiful. How do you tend to your duties with views such as this?"

"Tain't nothin', Miss, when you sees it day in an' day out fer months on end. The purser has a space on deck for yeh. It's outta the main. The crew ought not bother yeh here."

He led me to a cargo hatch toward the rear of the ship, atop of which a table and chair had been placed. A canvas tarp erected over the area provided shade. A wooden box sat at one side of the hatch as a step to permit easier access to the top. The chair was placed to allow views from both sides of the ship.

"Oh, Bert, this is a lovely spot. Please thank the purser for me." I settled in the chair, placed the parasol on the table, and opened the book. "I believe I shall be able to while away many hours here. I shan't keep you from your duties."

"For this watch, Miss, yeh are me duties. I shall niver be too far away. Jis give a haller if yeh need anythin'." He bowed and walked out of my sight.

I had no understanding of what he would do or how long his watch was. I resolved to ask Captain McClain when next I saw him.

I was absorbed in alternately looking about my new environment and reading when Bert came to escort me to dinner. It seemed only a few minutes but actually had been four hours. I found climbing down a ladder less cumbersome than going up, but still a challenge in maintaining proprieties.

Dinner passed pleasantly. Neither the captain nor I required a continuing dialog during the brief repast. Afterward, I returned to my cabin for the afternoon rest in which most ladies of means were obliged to indulge. I did not sleep but found the solitude of the cabin somewhat comforting.

Being accustomed to dressing for supper, I selected a burgundy silk dinner dress with a pearl brooch and earrings. A lace shawl and white gloves completed the ensemble.

Jacob Smythe appeared at my door at half past eight. He was a portly man with graying hair and striking blue eyes. His clothing was neat and clean. His words were sparse but indicated more than a perfunctory education.

By the third trip, the route to the wardroom had the feeling of familiarity. It was a great surprise to find the room crowded with gentlemen in varying degrees of formal attire. Some were in naval dress uniforms. Others wore swallowtail coats and canvas trousers. Still, others were wearing odd combinations of military and civilian evening attire. One gentleman was dressed in a swallowtail coat with knee breeches, complete with buckles at his knees and on his shoes. Yet another had donned trousers with a sack coat but no shoes or stockings. The odor of unwashed male bodies hung in the air.

The captain, wearing a well-tailored, immaculately clean white naval dress uniform, appeared at my side. The fragrance of bay rum lingered about him. He took my elbow and guided me to the chair to the right of his place at the head of the table. "It is tradition for the officers and midshipmen of the *Emma* to dine together our first night at sea. We do not usually dress formally, but it is not often a lovely lady graces our table."

"Thank you for the compliment, sir. I should think it rare for any woman to be at your table." It was an audacious remark to make to a person I had met that morning. But he laughed and conceded the truth of my statement.

"These gentlemen will ensure word is spread from topsails to bilge that you are to be treated with respect."

He sat, and the others quickly took their places.

The meal was served with the grace and expertise found in houses of the gentry. The supper was grander than the previous two meals. I surmised it was owing to this being our first night at sea.

Without calling attention to themselves, the men quit the wardroom by ones and twos. As the last officers left, the captain invited me to take a turn around the deck and led me to his private staircase.

The ocean air had cooled with the setting of the sun. The moon was rising, admiring itself in the reflection it made on the waters. Though I grew up on a farm, I had never seen so many stars. We stood at the railing, keeping our own counsel. Men went about their duties around us. Captain McClain scolded a young sailor when contents of the slop pail he was carrying spilled over, narrowly missing my dress.

Stifling a yawn, I said, "I believe it is time for me to retire for the evening. If you will be so good as to ask Jacob to escort me, I am sure you have important matters requiring your attention."

"Jacob is unavailable." His response seemed stilted and rehearsed. "I have assigned myself the task of seeing you safely below deck."

Opening the door to the cabin, Captain McClain handed me a key. "I realized this afternoon that no one gave you the key to this cabin. I apologize for the oversight."

"Thank you, Captain. For everything. I shall look forward to seeing you on the morrow." I entered the cabin and secured the door against intruders.

I was pleasantly exhausted after my first day at sea. As I nestled under the quilts, I resolved to reconsider my opinion of traveling on the water.

Chapter 3

Mine was a solitary existence despite there being fifty other souls on board. I quickly fell into a daily routine: Morning and mid-day meals were most often eaten alone in the wardroom. Mornings were spent on deck, enjoying fresh air before the heat of the day. Afternoons, I preferred the seclusion of my cabin. Captain McClain usually joined me for supper and proved to be an agreeable dining companion. Having no responsibilities, I filled my days with reading, sewing, and writing in my journal.

I cherished my time on deck and made a game of identifying the various odors wafting on the breezes. I watched fish jump out of the sea, and I learned the language of the seamen by watching and listening to the crew.

Bert taught me to tell time by the watch bells. "The helmsman keeps a sandglass an' rings the bell ever half hour. Even peals tell the hour. Odd uns er fer the half-hour. The most bells yeh'll hear are eight, fer the end of watch at four, eight, and twelve. Ever'un stands four-hour watches."

Contemplating my future was a frequent pastime. I imagined life with men I had seen visiting my father. Some imaginings were more pleasant than others. I was angry with Papa for arranging this marriage without my knowledge or consent. He expected I would honor the bargain without question. Yet, I did question it.

Ethan Brandt was frequently in my thoughts. I wondered whether my love for him would fade with time. *Would I ever love Josiah Pennyman?* Perhaps a fondness for him would grow.

As the ship moved farther from New England, realization dawned that this journey did not have to conclude with a wedding. It was within my power to choose my own future. I began considering whether I should marry this man or disembark before the ship reached my destination. I had no independent income, which led me to another quandary: *Should I choose the latter, how would I support myself?*

Fair weather blessed us the first days of the voyage. We had been at sea just short of a week. I was sitting on deck, stitching a rent in a glove, when a gust of wind pushed my mending basket across the table. As I snatched the basket from the table's edge, I became aware of the crew shouting and bustling about the ship. Sails were being hauled down, and halyards and ropes were being secured. Buckets and other loose equipment were being tucked away.

The wind was increasing. Dark clouds had gathered overhead. Forked lightning could be seen reaching into the water in the distance. With the scent of rain in my nose, I determined it prudent to return to my cabin before the storm broke.

I called to Bert. No response. I waited a few moments and called to him again, with the same result. Unable to locate Bert and not wanting to be caught on deck when the clouds released their burden, I resolved to take myself below.

Clutching the basket to my bosom, I negotiated the ladder and was making my way down the passage leading to my cabin when I saw a crewman coming toward me. Anticipating he would continue past me on his errand, I stopped and pressed myself and my dress as close to the wall as possible.

As he came nearer, I recognized him as the crewman who had shown me to the cabin when I first boarded the *Emma*. I had not seen him since that night and was unsettled about his being in this corridor.

Reaching out to me with both hands as he approached, he said, "Ah, m'lady is unescorted. Shall I see her to her quarters?"

A shudder coursed through my body. His leering eyes and smirking mouth belied the honey-sweet tone in his voice.

"I am quite capable of finding my way, thank you." I hoped I sounded braver than I felt. The space between us was rapidly shrinking. The fetid odor of his unwashed body and clothes swept over me.

"I tol yeh when yeh came aboard wemen hae nawt be on a ship." His tone turned menacing. He thrust his face into mine. "Time fer yeh to larn that."

His breath stank of spirits and rotting teeth. I trembled from the top of my bonnet to the tips of my boots. My mind raced, but I could think of nothing to say or do to stop him.

He snatched the basket from my hands and flung it aside. Its contents littered the floor of the passageway.

"Yeh'll hae naught use fer that." He sneered as his grimy hands clamped onto my upper limbs.

I held onto the wooden handrail in an effort to keep my feet under me. Tears welled in my eyes and spilled down my cheeks. He pulled me away from the wall and shoved me to the deck. Sitting on my nether limbs, he fumbled with his pants buttons. I pushed on his chest with my hands in an effort to unseat him.

"M'lady hae a bit o' the pluck in 'er," he growled through clenched teeth. "We'll soon remedy that." He swatted my hands away. The back of my gloved right hand hit something hard and metallic. Scissors. Twisting my right hand, I grasped them. He made guttural, animal sounds, all the while pushing his way through my underpinnings. Squeezing my eyes shut, I thrust the short, sharp blades of the embroidery scissors into his thigh.

Yelping an expletive, he captured my wrist with one hand whilst pulling the scissors from his leg and tossing them over his shoulder with the other. I heard fabric tear as he clawed at my chemise. He violently shoved my limbs apart with his knees.

Skirt fabric clung to my tear-drenched face. I feared for my life and fervently prayed for a swift death.

An exclamation of surprise escaped his lips, and his weight was lifted from my body. I pushed the skirts down in time to see the depraved man stumbled backward along the companionway. His trousers were settled around his ankles. Blood oozed down his left leg from the wound I had inflicted. The back of his head hit a wall, and the ruffian landed in a heap on the floor.

"Stay put, Crenshaw," Jacob shouted. "I shall deal with you directly." Turning toward me, fire still in his eyes, he asked, "Did he hurt you? Where's Bert?" His voice was quiet and comforting.

Through racking sobs, I explained as he helped me to my feet.

"Let's get you to your cabin. I'll be sure this blackguard is dealt with properly." Jacob tenderly supported my elbow and guided me to my cabin. I was shaking uncontrollably. He took the key from my hand and opened the door. Stepping inside behind me, he placed the key on the table and left, closing the door softly.

I secured the door, threw myself on the bed, and wept until exhaustion overtook me.

Chapter 4

The storm was raging when I awoke. Violent rolling and pitching of the ship had long since caused most everything on the table to be dashed to the floor. My boxes and trunks shifted with every movement. Shadows lurked in the corners, chased away by flashes of lightning. Rain sheeted down the tiny window. Thunder cracked overhead. I could hear the shouts of the sailors. Angrily creaking and moaning, the ship resisted the storm's attempts to break her asunder.

Crenshaw's menacing face surfaced in my mind's eye as I lay on the bed, his voice pounding in my ears, drowning out the storm. I made no effort to staunch the tears. I hugged the pillow tightly.

Loud rapping on the door startled me. I pulled out the handkerchief tucked in my sleeve and dabbed at my face. I eased off the bed, feet first, trying to stay upright. Pushing trunks and boxes out of my path, I cautiously took the few steps to the door, holding onto whatever was available.

"Who is there?" I called through the closed door, wary of who might be on the other side.

"It's Bert, Miss. I'm dreadful sorry fer not bein' close this mornin'. I was attendin' to pressin' matters in the fo'c'sle."

Unlocking and opening the door, I found the forlorn-looking sailor soaked to the skin. The hat in his hands dripped into a growing puddle under his bare feet.

"Was you damaged, Miss?"

"No, just frightened. Please, do not blame yourself."

"Durin' the forenoon watch me only duty was ter keep yeh safe. I failed. I'm awful sorry."

He wore his distress like an ill-fitting suit of clothes. My anguish diminished in my concern for his welfare.

"I knew I was not to leave the deck unescorted. I should have waited for you. The blame falls to me."

"Bless yeh, Miss. I fear the cap'n ain't so fergivin'." Rummaging in a pocket, he pulled out a wadded sheet of paper. "The cap'n said I was ta give this ta yeh and wait fer yer answer." He thrust the damp missive toward me.

The door swung closed when I released it. I moved to the table, leaving Bert to wait in the companionway. Finding a box of lucifers by a flash of lightning, I lit the wall lamp and smoothed out the damp paper to read the smudged handwriting.

Miss Llewellyn,

I am distressed to learn that you were accosted by one of my crewmen this morning. Be assured that swift and sure punishment shall be meted out.

I have grave concerns that you may have suffered injury during the ordeal. Do you require the services of the ship's surgeon?

I shall order the steward to serve you supper in your cabin.

Your servant,
Captain Ian McClain

I reread the message. It was heartwarming to know the captain's concern for my well-being. At the same time, I was disquieted at his having taken time to write it while laboring to keep the ship in one piece and on course. With great difficulty, I penned my reply on fresh stationery.

Captain McClain,

Thank you for your kind concern for my welfare. I am unharmed, though my nerves are frayed. There is no need to take the doctor from his responsibilities to tend to me.

Please, do not send your steward with a supper tray, as my appetite has abandoned me.

Respectfully,
Priscilla Llewellyn

I folded the page twice before opening the door. Handing my note to Bert, I told him I would not require an escort to supper. I needed time to collect myself. I'd venture out for breakfast if the storm had abated. I had no intention of allowing the actions of one ruffian to defeat me.

I passed a restless night. The storm subsided sometime in the early morning hours. I awoke to sunshine streaming through the window and the gentle rolling of calm seas. Forcing myself out of bed, I began returning order to the cabin. As I picked up a petticoat, the ruined chemise fluttered to the floor. Frozen in place, I stood and looked at it, tears falling on the cotton garment.

Picking up the looking glass, I gave myself a stern talking to about comportment. The reflection in the glass was not one I recognized. My face was puffy and blotchy, eyes red from crying and lack of sleep. "You must be strong," I said aloud to the face in the mirror, "You cannot show weakness in front of all these men."

Upon entering the wardroom for breakfast, I was surprised to find Captain McClain seated at the table. He was unshaven, with unkempt hair, and still wearing damp, soiled clothing. It was obvious he, too, had passed a sleepless night.

I served myself from the sideboard and slipped into my usual chair. An awkward silence followed stilted morning greetings. He finished his meal, poured a cup of coffee, and slouched on the edge of the table to my right.

"Miss Llewellyn, I would like you to pack your trunks. Be ready to have them moved to new quarters by two bells."

A quick computation told me I needed to be packed by 1:00 p.m.

"It was my error that put you in danger, and I mean to rectify it," he continued.

"Sir, you are by no means responsible for the actions of a superstitious heathen. I hold no animosity toward you."

"This ship, her crew, and her cargo are my responsibility. It was ill-advised of me to select a cabin for you so near the crew quarters. I should have anticipated you would encounter one of our more unsavory companions."

"Am I to presume my new quarters will be a packing crate?" I teased. I knew I should be serious, but it was difficult when he referred to me as 'cargo.'

"If passage is paid, it is 'cargo,'" he sighed. "I do not believe you have been treated in the same manner as the cargo stored in the hold. Your luggage is to be moved to a cabin nearer the stern."

"Thank you, Sir. I am sorry to be a nuisance."

"You are far from a nuisance." A smile touched his lips for just a moment. He shook his head. "I have granted passage to other women who were thorns in my side from the moment they came aboard till the moment they went ashore and then continued their diatribe through correspondence." He suppressed a shudder.

"I assure you, I have learned this lesson well. I shall be on my best behavior and will not wander about unattended again."

He smiled and chuckled. "That is most gratifying and unnecessary. The crew witnessed Crenshaw's punishment after the storm passed. I shall spare you the unsavory details. I do not believe you will have to endure further unpleasant encounters with any of the remaining crew. The incident shall not be spoken of again." He finished drinking his coffee, placed the cup on the table, and walked out of the room, leaving me alone.

Chapter 5

The *Emma* was our floating island. While at sea, we lived an isolated, feudal existence. The crew was paid to do the commander's bidding. I was on this ship at the pleasure of the same man. Fleetingly, I wondered whether the captain ever thought of me as anything other than cargo.

Life on the ship resumed its usual pace. Jacob told me we were now south of the Mason-Dixon Line. We were close enough to see the coastline on the starboard side. This was the first time I had been this far south.

Like most people, I had read about General Sherman's March to the Sea during the winter of 1864 and the destruction his army had left in their wake. Ethan had written to me when his regiment was reassigned to General Sherman. Pride shown through his words as he wrote of his regiment being the first Union force to enter Atlanta. He wrote of the hardships suffered by the Southern people left behind after battles and skirmishes.

I wondered whether the Southerners would ever be able to rebuild their former lives.

A change in the crew's behavior occurred shortly before the appearance of a series of islands on the port side. There was no more jocularity among the men. They spoke in subdued tones and peered into the sea with a mixture of reverence and trepidation writ across their faces.

Observing these phenomena during the morning watches, I was overcome with curiosity. As Jacob escorted me from the deck to the wardroom for dinner, I asked him what the men were looking at.

"These be queer waters, Miss. Many a ship has met her doom hereabouts. 'Tis bad luck to speak of such things." He made the sign of the cross and muttered under his breath whilst quickening his step.

Several men were seated around the table when I entered the wardroom. The talk was earnest but hushed, leading me to believe something was amiss. The meeting disbanded soon after my arrival, leaving the ship's master and me to dine alone.

"Good afternoon, Captain. To what do I owe the pleasure of your company?" I smiled.

"We are entering waters that require a good bit of seamanship. Slumber will be elusive, and meals sparse for the crew and myself the next few days."

"Jacob told me these were queer waters, but they look quite ordinary."

"Ah, yes." He rolled his eyes toward the ceiling. "Most of the crew are seasoned sailors." He paused. "And quite superstitious. I wouldn't put a great deal of stock in their ramblings." The tone of his voice and the look on his face belied his words.

"Methinks you are not being wholly truthful. I've observed the men on deck. Their comport is unsettled. Your crew is clearly troubled by something. I would like to understand why."

Taking a bite of pork stew, he looked at his plate, then across the table at me. "There are legends about strange occurrences hereabout. The route we are taking is challenging, but not because of the bunkum in those tales."

His explanation was sensible, but I was unwilling to allow the subject to lie. "It appears that the waters we are entering manifest fascination. The crew is spending an extraordinary amount of time looking for something in the sea. I want to understand why everyone is behaving so peculiarly. I have no desire to be coddled or treated as a simpleton."

"Petulance does not become you, Miss Llewellyn." He sighed. "There are some who believe these waters bewitched. There are fanciful tales of ships disappearing, never to be seen or heard from again. Some believe there to be merpeople in these waters. Others are keeping watch for sirens or other demons wishing to entice them into the sea and a watery death." He swallowed his wine in one long draught. "It's all humbug, but there you have it.

"We shall soon enter the shallow waters of the Florida Keys. The crew and I have safely navigated through them many times. However, it requires a great deal of skill to maneuver the coral that lies on the seafloor. Many a ship has had her hull torn asunder on those coral reefs." He brought his napkin to his face. Throwing it down as he rose from his chair, he stated, "I shall now take my leave. Good afternoon, Miss Llewellyn." He strode toward the staircase.

Tension on the ship was thick as fog. The only talk on deck was that required to convey orders or provide information regarding the position of the ship in relation to the reefs over which we crept and the depth of the water. Over the succeeding days, the sailors spent part of their day standing at the railing and staring into the sea. I succumbed to curiosity and took my turn there. What I saw was wondrous.

The shallow water was clear as window glass. Fish swam alongside and under the *Emma*. The majesty of the coral was breathtaking. The ship glided over the jagged formations. I shuddered as one brushed the side of the ship and gave me to understand the dangers we faced should the ship become impaled by them.

The coral wasn't our only obstacle. We witnessed half-dressed men swimming and crawling through carcasses of ships that had wrecked on the coral. I watched with rapt interest as a man disappeared through a large hole in a ship's hull and returned with men in tow—crewmen who had been unable to escape a watery death. Others dismantled rigging whilst another group disappeared into the ship to return with crates from the hold.

Jacob walked by my deck space as I watched the men work on the broken and battered ship. "It is a sight to see, is it not, Miss?"

"Indeed, Jacob. It is quite humbling to realize that we might succumb to a similar fate. I am pleased this industry is back with the United States."

"Oh, Miss, the salvaging has always been in the hands of the Union. Ships have been wrecking on the coral reefs for longer than anyone knows. The government has long known of the wealth to be had from the holds of these ships. These men live on the Keys over yonder." He nodded toward the workers on the spoiled ship and pointed toward an island not far from our position. "President Lincoln posted extra troops at the navy base and built two more forts to keep hold of these islands.

"I heard that Dr. Mudd, that fellow who helped out John Wilkes Booth, was sent to Fort Jefferson on Dry Tortugas. That's that island over yonder." Jacob pointed to a landmass some distance away.

“Sorry to run off, Miss, but I am on an errand,” Jacob said over his shoulder as he dashed toward the prow.

We had been inching over the coral reefs for two days. It was late morning of the third day as I sat on the deck, lost in flights of fancy. A figure blocked the sun, casting a shadow over me. I was pleasantly surprised to find the captain on deck. He looked fatigued but was dressed in clean clothes.

"Pardon the intrusion, Miss Llewellyn. Would you honor me with a stroll around the deck?" he asked, a smile playing on his lips.

"Captain McClain, what a pleasant surprise. I should be pleased to stroll with you." Closing the book in my lap and placing it on the table, I took up my parasol and placed my hand on his proffered forearm.

The sky was blue and the sea calm. There was sufficient breeze to fill the shortened sails but not so robust as to blow one about the deck. The ribbon ties on my bonnet fluttered about like moths near a flame.

“Am I to surmise from your abandonment of the bridge that we are out of danger?”

“The ship is in no immediate danger. We should be shut of the reefs before the day is ended. Mr. Sudbroeker has taken command of the bridge.”

“I trust you shall be able to take to your berth ere long?”

“Aye, I shall soon enough.”

A companionable silence ensued as we watched a man, prone on the prow, feed a line into the water. As we continued our walk around the deck, there was a cry from the prow, "BY THE MARK: TEN.” The call was repeated in turn by several others.

A chill ran down my spine as I looked toward the sailor on the prow and then at the man at my side. A sense of relief swept over me as comprehension brought knowledge the coral reefs were behind us. We were safely in the Gulf of Mexico. This was a moment to be joyful.

The crew broke into cheers and danced about. I'd not seen such celebrating since word of General Lee's surrender had been received at our farm. The excitement was infectious, and I found myself smiling, then laughing. My left hand rested on the railing, and I became aware of a weight atop it. I looked down to see Captain McClain's hand covering mine.

It felt nice. It felt right. But I was betrothed to another. Reluctantly, I started to pull my hand away.

Feeling the movement, Captain McClain said, "I beg your pardon, Miss Llewellyn. I meant no disrespect."

"And none was perceived."

Impulsively, the captain grabbed my right hand in his left and placed his right hand on my waist. We danced a polka some twenty feet down the deck. Then, just as suddenly, we stopped dancing and began to walk as though nothing had happened. We both laughed heartily as sailors gaped at their captain's uncharacteristic behavior.

The celebration lasted just a few minutes. It seemed as though the crew knew exactly how long they were allowed to express their joy and relief before they would be admonished to return to their duties.

"Do I perceive an ulterior motive for our stroll?" I asked.

"I do not know how such a notion came into your mind," he replied in mock innocence.

Exchanging small talk, we eventually returned to my little space on the deck. There, we found dinner for two laid and waiting for us.

“My, you truly are a man of surprises today.” I was delighted at the opportunity to dine on deck and to be in Captain McClain’s company.

He silently held the chair for me.

Chapter 6

My new cabin was nearer the wardroom. Though similarly furnished, it was larger and more opulently decorated than the former. After overhearing men talk about soon being in New Orleans, I wondered whether my time on the *Emma* may be coming to an end.

As I lay on the bed after dinner, thoughts, and memories flitted through my mind like butterflies in a meadow on a spring day. Unpleasant memories were pushed aside. Lingering in the back of my mind were thoughts of Captain McClain. He was tall and handsome and a consummate gentleman. The few polka steps on deck proved that he had promise as a dance partner. He appeared to be well-educated. His clothing was that of a gentleman.

I hope and pray that my betrothed possesses half his qualities. He is easy to talk with and listens when I speak. He is a stern but fair master...I wonder whether there is a Mrs. Captain McClain.

Reluctantly, I pushed these thoughts aside to ruminate upon my fate of marrying a complete stranger. Despite a strong desire to abandon all and make a different life for myself, I resolved to continue my journey to marry the man my father had chosen for me. But I wanted to prevent my future husband from gaining possession of the family heirlooms now resting in the hold.

Sounds from above deck were muted in this cabin. I could only faintly hear the watch bell tolling seven bells. A glance at my timepiece jolted me back to reality. I quickly but carefully dressed for supper and was ready when my escort arrived.

The captain and I had finished supper and were savoring a bread pudding. Desserts and confections were a rarity on the *Emma*. Conversation had been sparse during the meal.

"We will be docking in New Orleans early tomorrow morning," the ship's master informed me.

I gathered the courage to ask the question foremost on my mind. "Am I to be put off the ship?"

"You are free to go ashore, should you insist. But this city is not your destination. We shall be in port for several days. There is business to transact and fresh supplies to take on. The ship requires repairs best made in port."

"It will be nice to walk on solid ground again. And I should like to do some shopping."

The captain continued, "I do not believe the wharf to be safe for a lady to traverse alone. The citizens are having a difficult time transitioning from the Union occupation to a civilian government. I believe it best that someone accompanies you to the business district. I caution you to be very careful."

"Before leaving Connecticut, I read newspaper accounts of difficulties in the South. Four years of killing and maiming seems insufficient for the most rebellious. I promise to be on my best behavior."

"Jacob will meet you here in the morning." Silence again engulfed us as we ate the last of the pudding. Abruptly, Captain McClain stood and asked, "Shall we take a bit of air on deck?"

Chapter 7

The ship was already docked when I awoke. Sailors were going about their work, making a dreadful din that could be heard in my cabin. After weeks at sea, the crew was excited to be going ashore as soon as the *Emma* was properly secured to the dock and cargo had been withdrawn from the bowels of the ship.

Jacob, followed by Robert Boleyn, entered the wardroom as I lingered over a cup of tea. Jacob's appearance was markedly changed. He had exchanged his sea clothing for inexpensive but handsome brown trousers and sack coat, a white shirt, and a startlingly bright green tie. His hair was combed and pomaded, and his beard neatly trimmed. Robert was similarly attired, though his sack coat was a little too large, and his tie was a sedate black.

Robert stood next to Jacob, fidgeting.

"Stand still, boy," Jacob commanded.

"It's these clothes, sir," Robert protested. "They're binding my limbs."

"You are quite well turned out," I commented. "I scarcely recognized either of you."

"Thank you, Miss," they responded in unison.

"It seems the prospect of going ashore has everyone in high spirits this morning," I observed.

"That is a fact, Miss," Jacob replied. "Don't rush your meal. We will wait for you in the passageway."

“Thank you, Jacob,” I said, pushing away from the table and standing. “I have finished breaking my fast. Allow me to retrieve some things from my cabin before we disembark.”

New Orleans residents had burned ships and much of the wharf in 1861 to prevent the Union from gaining control of them for their own use. The usual loading and unloading of cargo and passengers, combined with the construction of new docks and warehouses, made negotiating the wharf hazardous. We picked our way through the congestion, finally setting our feet on firm land.

The city was relatively undamaged during the Rebellion. Most destruction to the city had been at the hands of its citizens in anticipation of Northern occupation. The United States Army had occupied the city since April 1862.

The residents were resentful and antagonistic toward the Union troops. Equipped with this knowledge, I was uncertain whether the shopkeepers would be friendly to this Northern lady.

While still on the outskirts of the city, I enquired, “Jacob, would you have time to meet me for tea this afternoon? I have something I wish to discuss with you. In private.”

“You sure I’m the right person to talk with?”

“I have given this matter a great deal of thought. You are the only person I am able to talk with about it. It would not be appropriate to speak of this with Captain McClain. I hope you can find it in your heart to help me.”

“I will be occupied with ship business until the start of the dog watch.”

“My errands should be completed by then. Do you know New Orleans well? Is there a tea shop where we might meet?”

"Aye, Miss. I recollect seeing a tea shop on Peters Street, near the French Market. Young Robert, here, knows the way."

"Then it is settled. We shall meet at the tea shop on Peters Street at four this afternoon."

Our conversation had brought us to the business district. "I shall leave you here, Miss. Do be mindful of your whereabouts. Robert, you make sure no harm comes to Miss Llewellyn," Jacob cautioned as he turned into a side street and disappeared into the crowd.

Fears that my New England accent would cause a poor reception were unfounded. However, I do speculate that the gold and silver coins withdrawn from my reticule were the primary reason for the favorable service rendered by the shopkeepers.

Reports I had read of unrest in the city were severely understated. New Orleans was, indeed, a powder keg waiting to be ignited. Men and women with leaflets stood at street corners, proclaiming their causes to whoever would stop to listen. Most moved past them with eyes averted, simply wanting to complete their errands and return to their homes. Tempers flared at the slightest provocation. Loud arguments in an odd mixture of French and English were commonplace. Drays and coaches were forced to drive around street fights or run over pugilists. It was evident that the flame would be put to the fuse sooner than later. I kept to myself, speaking only with shop clerks or Robert.

Our first destination was *The Bank of New Orleans*. I presented letters of introduction and credit from Father's bank in Connecticut. My business was soon completed, and my young companion and I proceeded to the shops.

In need of a new spring bonnet, I went to a milliner's shop. An attractive young lady assisted me in finding the perfect one. A bit of translucent silk skillfully draped over it transformed the bonnet into the crowning touch to my wedding attire. While lovingly placing it in a hatbox, she recommended a lovely little restaurant where I might take my mid-day meal.

We had no difficulty in locating the restaurant. Robert followed the hostess to a table and deposited my parcels in a vacant chair. Once assured that I was settled, he followed the woman to a back room where he was fed. I enjoyed my first meal away from the ship in close to a month.

After paying for our meals, I found Robert in front of the restaurant, playing with a bandalore. After winding the string between the discs and stuffing the toy in a pocket, he took the parcels from me, and we began our walk toward Peters Street.

I was nervous being on the streets. Fights broke out for little or no reason. Men lounging nearby readily joined in, creating large crowds of brawling men and women. I feared being swept into one of these melees. I insisted Robert enter shops with me to distance ourselves from the turmoil. He expressed reluctance to do so but seemed relieved to be out of the fray.

Happening upon a bookstore, I spent more time than intended browsing the shelves for tomes that talked to me. Out of the corner of my eye, I watched Robert tentatively pick up several volumes, leaf through them, and replace them on the shelves with great reverence. We left the bookstore with a rather heavy parcel added to Robert's burden. He bore it well, without complaint or comment. I am sure he would have rather been anywhere within the city than shopping with me. Hearing a church bell chime half past three, I feared being late for my appointment.

We arrived at *Maribelle's Tea Shop* before Jacob. I secured a table near the large window facing the street. After practically dropping the parcels into an empty chair, Robert dashed outside to wait until Jacob put his hand on the doorknob. Robert and Jacob exchanged words, and Robert left at a run.

Jacob approached the table, voicing concern that he had kept me waiting. I assured him that was not the case. A kind woman with silver-gray hair took our order.

We shared dainties and a pot of Earl Gray tea. After a lengthy discussion, he agreed to the favor I asked of him, the magnitude of which I might never be able to repay.

The ship was nearly deserted when Jacob and I returned. Only the crewmen on watch and those occupied with the repairs were on board. I was pleasantly exhausted from my day in the city.

At the door of my cabin, I opened my reticule and counted out several banknotes, which I handed to Jacob.

"This should be more than sufficient. But, if you find it is not, please tell me."

Jacob took the money, folded it in half, and shoved it into a pocket. "Don't you give it another thought, miss. I'll get it done before we leave port."

"I don't know how to repay your kindness," I said before crossing the threshold into my cabin.

After eight days in The Port of New Orleans, repairs were completed, cargo secured below decks, the hatch covers were battened down, and my table and chair were restored to their accustomed place. I stood at the rail for one last look at New Orleans as a steam-powered tug boat pulled the *Emma* toward open water. Some of the crew were in high spirits, while others were obviously feeling the ill effects of their low living while ashore.

A deceptive appearance of calm belied the truth of the turmoil in the city streets, taverns, hotels, and homes. There was no single or simple solution to the problems these citizens faced. There was to be no easy death for slavery. Generations of treating the Negros worse than they treated their livestock or pets could not be unlearned with the stroke of President Lincoln's forever silent and dry pen.

I found myself becoming melancholy as the ship sailed toward the setting sun. The days grew longer and warmer as the calendar hurtled toward the summer solstice. I spent more time on deck, finding it easier to pass the afternoons with the unacknowledged companionship of the working men than in the solitary confines of my cabin.

We had been under sail for four days when I overheard Mr. Sudbroeker and Jacob talk about being at our destination the next day. The realization that I would soon be a married lady sent all the old misgivings and doubt to crowd my thoughts. *Should I marry this man? Should I refuse to leave the ship?*

No, I told myself. *Continue with your plan. Try to postpone the wedding. Become acquainted with this Josiah Pennyman before you commit to spending a lifetime with him. If necessary, feign illness.*

The day passed quietly, and the coastline grew nearer. Captain McClain held a supper party in my honor. I found myself making comparisons to that first dinner party nearly a month earlier, with the officers and midshipmen dressed in their odd versions of formal attire.

The conversation was lively, all of us more comfortable than that night seemingly a lifetime ago. As with that other supper, after the meal was consumed and the port had been drunk, the men drifted away to their watches or to take to their bunks.

Left alone, the captain and I indulged in one last stroll on deck. After a long silence, the captain stated, "You are an uncommon woman, Miss Llewellyn."

The sentiment startled me. I never thought of myself as anything but plain and ordinary. "Thank you, Captain. What has transpired to lead you to that conclusion?"

"I had been told you were no lover of ships and the sea. I expected a torrent of complaints from the moment you boarded the *Emma*. Yet, I've heard nary a one from you."

"Would my circumstances have changed had I complained? With certain exceptions, you and your crew have been kind and considerate. My days onboard your ship have been wonderfully comfortable. I have no reason to complain about that which cannot be changed, nor what I do not find unpleasant."

"I am pleased that you have found us tolerable."

“Indeed, I have become quite fond of Bert and Jacob, particularly. They both proved loyal during my darkest hours on this ship.”

“Bert was derelict in his duty that day.” Anger crept into his voice. “He has yet to redeem himself in my eyes.”

“Please, do not punish him. I am certain he had good reason to be away from his post. He told me he had urgent business in the forecastle, though I have no knowledge of what that would be.”

The captain’s broad smile and soft chuckle puzzled me. “I suppose I cannot punish a man for answering the call of nature,” he chortled.

Glad for the darkness, I felt myself blush. I had somehow remained ignorant of what duties were performed in the forecastle until that moment.

We completed our turn around the deck. He saw me to my cabin and walked toward his own, muttering something about his pillow.

Chapter 8

The morning sun shone through the small window in my cabin. I had packed the last of my possessions after completing my morning ablutions. With nothing to occupy my mind or hands, I stood at the rail and watched the ship move toward the harbor. *I shall meet Mr. Pennyman before the sun drops below the horizon.* I had indulged in speculation as to his appearance and demeanor several times a day since Papa told me of the bargain he had made. I made every effort to refrain from further cogitation. Gentleman or scoundrel, Josiah Pennyman's true nature would soon be known.

My knowledge of geography west of the Mississippi River was severely lacking. I was reasonably certain we were still within the United States, but which state? Captain McClain had steadfastly kept his promise to my father until this moment.

"You are gazing upon Corpus Christi, Texas." The captain's voice startled me.

Deep in my musings, I had not heard him come to stand next to me.

"I'm not sure how to feel about disembarking. I find myself reluctant to leave the ship." I looked up at him.

"But, you are no lover of the sea," he teased. The *Emma*'s commander sobered, looking straight ahead at the small boats docked at the wharf. "Mr. Pennyman is a man of means."

"Are you acquainted with him?"

"Only by reputation. I have never been introduced to him."

"What do you know of him?" The pitch of my voice rose in relation to my anxiety.

As he opened his mouth to respond, Robert ran toward us, stopping short of crashing headlong into his employer. Gulping for breath, the boy panted, "Sir, Mr. Sudbroeker requests your presence on the quarterdeck."

"Inform the first officer I shall be there forthwith." Pivoting on his heel, the captain bowed, "By your leave, Miss Llewellyn."

Once more left to my own devices, I wished I had thought to keep out a book to read during these last hours on board. Time moved slowly.

There being no deep-water port, The *Emma* anchored some distance offshore. The hold was opened, and cargo brought to the deck while a number of shallow-draft boats made their way to our watery mooring. Crates and barrels were transferred to these lighters to continue their journey to Corpus Christi Bay.

The crew bustled about the ship, stowing equipment, securing sails, and the myriad of other tasks required to secure the ship while at anchor. I did my best to stay out of the way while searching the boats flocking to our vessel for anyone who looked as though he might be Josiah Pennyman.

I saw Robert Boleyn dashing about the deck, talking to this sailor and that crewman. I hoped to wish him Godspeed before I left the ship. The opportunity came just as a barge pulled alongside the *Emma*.

"Robert," I called. "May I have a moment of your time, please?"

The boy stopped short in front of me. "Yes, Miss?"

"I wanted to say how very pleased I am to have made

your acquaintance and thank you for escorting me through New Orleans."

"Twern't nothin', Miss. I was just doin' what Mr. Smythe told me to do, s'all."

"Well, I thought you very brave and am most appreciative that you carried my parcels about town."

The boy showed signs of impatience, dancing from one foot to the other and looking about the deck.

"I want you to have this," I finished and shoved a small parcel at the boy.

He looked surprised but tentatively put out a hand to take the gift and looked at it with wonder. "Thank you, Miss."

"Please, open it," I encouraged.

He looked up, then tore open the brown paper. Inside lay a volume of *The Pioneers,* written by James Fennimore Cooper, I had seen him perusing in the New Orleans bookshop.

The boy looked up, his eyes sparkling. "Thank you, Miss. No one ever gave me my own book afore. I'll keep it forever." He took several steps and turned, "Thank you, Miss. Goodbye."

With that, the boy ran toward the bow of the ship and was lost in the crush of sailors.

It was late afternoon when a man dressed in clean but tattered Confederate butternut ascended from one of these boats. After clambering up the boarding ladder, he stood on the deck near the cookhouse and bellowed, "Is there a Miss Priscilla Llewellyn aboard?"

A disembodied voice from above returned, "Who be askin'?"

"Major Percival Templeton." His Southern accent rang clearly. "My employer has dispatched me to call for the woman." The man waved an envelope in the direction of the voice.

"Stay where ye be," the anonymous voice called from somewhere in the rigging.

I watched and listened to this exchange from near the bow, hidden from view of the former Confederate officer by a longboat. I did not see from what direction he came, but Mr. Sudbroeker soon stood before the visitor. I moved closer to the deckhouse for better vantage.

The conversation between the two men was lost to me as they spoke in low tones. The envelope, proffered by the stranger, was accepted and opened by the first officer. Mr. Sudbroeker perused the contents, made a shallow bow, and took the steps leading to the quarterdeck two at a time. An interval of some minutes transpired, during which the Butternut Man, as I dubbed him in my mind, did not move but shifted his gaze about the ship. His eyes rested on me. His countenance visibly changed to that of a man with impure thoughts.

With some effort, I did not acknowledge his ogle. Rather, I espied movement behind him and fixed my eyes over his shoulder onto the kitchen mate assiduously scrubbing an enormous pot.

Captain McClain quit the quarterdeck with far less vigor than his first officer had ascended. He approached the visitor, envelope, and documents in hand.

The conversation was not particularly animated. The majority of movement comprised of shuffling papers and indicating passages on various sheets.

The Butternut Man's state of agitation mounted as the interview wore on. His face grew red, and his hands clenched and unclenched in an obvious effort to keep his temper under control.

Movement to my right caught my attention. Jacob

emerged from the hold. He craned his neck both right and left, looking about the deck. The interrogation taking place mid-ship caught his attention. Sidling closer to me, he observed, “The Reb looks none too comfortable. Have they been at it long?”

“They have been speaking for some minutes.”

“I wonder what the captain’s said to get him worked up.”

“I suspect the Butternut Man objects to anyone casting doubt on his authority. His comport makes me uneasy.”

“The captain will not allow you to leave with the Reb unless he is certain of the man’s veracity.”

Neither of us had taken our eyes off the conversing men.

Captain McClain exuded calm and control while the Butternut Man was losing his composure. If this interview continued overlong, I feared there would be violence.

As Jacob and I watched the scene down deck, I said, “I am indebted to you. Our talk in New Orleans has made today easier.”

“You certain you want it like this?” he enquired.

“It’s the only thing about which I am certain.” My attention returned to the two men determining my fate.

The captain stopped a crewman passing by on an errand. They exchanged a few words, and the sailor looked about as though searching for something or someone. Seeing Jacob and me, he spoke again to his commander, made an almost imperceptible nod, and made his way across the deck to where we were positioned.

“Mr. Smythe, Captain McClain requests you escort the lady to him,” the young man stated and resumed his original errand without waiting for a reply.

“Are you ready?” Jacob asked me.

“No, but there is nothing for it but to go through with what has been put into motion.”

He started to offer his arm, looked at the sleeve streaked with grease, glanced at me, and put his arm at his side as I fell into step beside him.

The captain made the introductions. The Butternut Man bent in a moderate bow at the waist but did not speak.

"How do you do, Mr. Templeton?" I said with all the politeness I could gather. I could not fathom the insolence exuding from this man. His expression reminded me of my father's when he assessed livestock.

Mr. Templeton completed his appraisal and turned his attention back to the ship's commander, "I trust the lady's baggage has been loaded onto the barge. We have been delayed overlong."

"It was loaded while we conversed," Captain McClain clipped his words. His back was ramrod straight, disapproval writ on his face. "If you will excuse me."

He turned to me, took my left hand, bowed deeply, and said, "Miss Llewellyn, my best wishes to you." He dropped my hand and walked back toward the quarterdeck.

Perceval Templeton was a man of average stature. He stood erect and carried himself with an arrogance that might be mistaken for confidence. It was obvious from his demeanor that he was unaccustomed to explaining himself. With nothing but his manner of looking upon me to base my discomfiture, I resolved to give him no reason to display whatever temper he may possess.

"Miss Llewellyn, it is time to leave," he stated.

"I am ready." I steeled myself to make the journey from ship to shore with this man.

The boatswain's chair had been connected to the rigging used to load cargo onto the lighters. Jacob helped me settle onto the weathered but clean board that sufficed for a seat and showed me how to hold the thick ropes to maintain my balance during the transfer from ship to lighter. It reminded me of the swing hanging from the old oak tree at *Riverbend*.

Once I was settled in the chair to Jacob's satisfaction, sailors heaved on the ropes, raising me above the height of the ship's railing. They swung the chair over the side and began the delicate procedure of lowering me onto the barge. The slightest movement set the chair to swinging back and forth. With the wind in my face, my feet coming ever closer to the deck of the lighter, and looking across to the people on the *Emma*, I began to laugh. I truly was cargo.

I would not allow myself to look at the *Emma* as the barge began its slow movement toward the shore. I sat on a crate with my back to the ship that had carried me so far from the only home I had known. I stared at the water and the coastline as the sun began its descent into the sea.

Long shadows stretched out ahead of me on the wharf when we finally docked. I identified my baggage, and Mr. Templeton directed the trunks and boxes to be taken away. I allowed myself one last glance at the *Emma*, now appearing so small at that distance. Tears began to well and threatened my composure. I sighed, blinked the salty water from my eyes, and turned toward the harbor.

With trepidation, I followed Percival Templeton down the short dock to begin my new life.

PART 2
Gehenna

Chapter 9

May 1866
Corpus Christi, Texas

My baggage was loaded into a farm wagon positioned in front of a large warehouse on the wharf and laden with numerous crates, barrels, and parcels. Mr. Templeton climbed onto the teamster's seat without a word or look.

"If you're comin' with us, you best git in the wagon," he sneered over his shoulder.

I looked at the wagon in bewilderment. "How do I board this conveyance? And where am I to sit? It appears you are ensconced on the only seat available."

"Hie yourself up over the side and set where you can." Insolence dripped from each word.

"Is there no block upon which I may stand to gain access to the wagon?" I fought to keep my voice calm, a feat that was becoming increasingly difficult. I was unaccustomed to being treated in so coarse a manner.

The teamster overheard this entire discourse while making final adjustments to the harness that joined two black draft horses to the wagon. He looked at Mr. Templeton with undisguised contempt and walked around to the back of the wagon. Without speaking, he released the catches, pulled down the tailgate, heaved a box from the wagon bed, and placed it on the ground. After removing his heavy leather gloves, the gray-haired man offered his hand to me. I placed my gloved hand in his to steady myself as I stepped onto the box. From this new vantage point, I contemplated how best to enter the wagon.

"It'd be best to set yersef on the tail and swing yer limbs round, Miss," the teamster offered in a quiet voice.

"Thank you," I whispered and followed his instructions.

Gaining my feet and surveying the wagon bed from this new perspective, I located a spot I thought advantageous for remaining inside the wagon during what may prove to be a perilous trip. Having judiciously stepped through the wagon's load, I sank, squirmed about to find a comfortable position, and tucked in my skirts as best I could to avoid their fluttering about during the ride.

There were questions I wanted to ask but thought better of voicing them. *I shall ask them later,* I told myself. Mr. Templeton was obviously anxious for the journey to begin. I reasoned that his temperament was due to the lateness of the day and his desire to convey me to Mr. Pennyman before nightfall.

Corpus Christi was small, more of a village than a city. The streets were unpaved, the buildings constructed of wood or an odd-looking tan-colored brick. Union soldiers walked about, rifles casually slung over their shoulders. *Why are they here?* I pondered the question as we passed the last vestiges of civilization.

The unchanging landscape did not hold my interest. In stark contrast to the lush woods of New England, scrubby little bushes and stunted trees dotted the barren and coarse Texas landscape of rock and sand. I saw few birds or other animals, though I was confident they must be out there somewhere.

We were not far outside the city when the wagon veered to the right and stopped in a copse of trees growing beside a small stream. Both men jumped from their perch. The teamster unbuckled the harness and walked the horses to the stream.

Mr. Templeton walked around rubbing his backside and stretching. Not knowing the length of time we would be stopped, I stood and shook each lower limb in turn but made no effort to quit the wagon bed.

The two men talked quietly while the teamster hobbled the horses and removed the last of their tack. It was not until he came to the side of the wagon to fetch feed bags for the beasts that the teamster realized I had not descended.

"Did Templeton not tell you we would pass the night here?" he asked.

"No. I am afraid he did not think it necessary," I replied, shaken by this new development. I took no pleasure in the notion of passing the night on the side of a dirt track with the Butternut Man.

"Ah, yes. Mr. Templeton does play his cards close to the chest. We are still some distance from Gehenna. We'll strike out again at first light. Let me help you down from there." His voice was genial but left no doubt that he did not share the Butternut Man's proclivities.

He lowered the tailgate and waited while I wended my way through the maze of boxes and parcels toward him. I then sat on the tail and jumped, my skirts flouncing as I landed flat-footed on the dusty road.

"Thank you for your assistance. I do not believe we may depend on Mr. Templeton to make introductions. I am Miss Priscilla Llewellyn."

"Nice to know ya, Miss. They call me Gump Hoss."

"What an unusual name. How ever did you come by such an alias?"

He broke into a broad grin. "My grandson gave it to me.

When he was young, he liked to go to the stable to see me and the horses. One day, he got excited and mush-mouthed. I've been Gump Hoss ever since."

"Well, Gump Hoss, I'm pleased to make your acquaintance," an equally broad smile spread across my face.

He leaned in, close to my right ear, and whispered, "I reckon yeh need to tend to some needs. If'n yeh wander to'ther side of those trees, ya'll find a boulder. It should afford yeh some privacy."

My eyes followed the line from his pointed finger. "Thank you, Gump Hoss," I called over my shoulder as I hurriedly walked toward the trees.

The moon was on the rise when I passed through the widely spaced trees facing the wagon. A small fire was the only light. I made my way toward it.

Gump Hoss was feeding pieces of wood to the fire while Mr. Templeton lounged on a dirty blanket and watched. They had been talking but stopped when Templeton saw me at the edge of the circle of light.

I stood for a few moments, looking into the flames. A shiver coursed down my spine. I was uncertain whether it was due to the cooling air or the recumbent man in the Confederate uniform. I squared my shoulders and forced my feet to move closer.

"So, you decided to grace us with your presence, did you?" Percival Templeton lay on his side, head propped on his left hand. He held something in his right hand near his chest.

Gump Hoss moved quietly about the camp. He opened two jars and poured their contents into a pot. Balancing the pot on several rocks poking up through the burning wood, he stirred the contents in earnest. “Supper will be warm soon.” He looked at me with a sorrowful expression.

None of us spoke for some time, the hissing and popping of the fire the only sounds.

“Are yeh goin’ to set yerself down sometime, Missy? Yer gonna get awful tired standin’ like that.” The former Confederate wore his disgust like a mantle.

“I would sit, should there be something upon which to sit,” I glowered. “I am not in the habit of wallowing in soil.”

“Well, we seem to be a tad short on fine furniture. Ye’ll have to make do with what’s about,” Templeton sneered.

“A blanket or rug would do,” I countered. “Perhaps one of the boxes in the wagon?”

“Sit in the dirt. Or stand. Ain’t no never mind to me.” He continued to stare into the flames. He caressed the object in his right hand.

Gump Hoss gave the contents of the pot a stir and put another log on the fire. He appeared to take in the conversation but made no contribution to it. The grandfather went about his business competently. He walked past me into the darkness. Scraping noises could be heard, and he returned with a rough wool blanket in his hands.

“I don’t expect it’s too clean, but you’re welcome to settle yourself on it,” he said, spreading it out.

“Thank you, Gump Hoss. You are most kind,” I replied, perhaps a little too sweetly.

“Why you pamperin’ her, old man? She ain’t nothin’ but a spoiled rich chit.” Mr. Templeton’s displeasure was wrapped around each word. “She oughtta learn her place here and now. She ain’t gonna be coddled none when she gets to Gehenna.”

“Mind yersef, Templeton. I ‘spect yeh ain’t had much experience with the gentry. This here’s a lady. She don’t get treated like them fancy women of yer's down ta saloon." Derision rang in every word he spoke. "You leave her be. You lay one finger on her, and Mr. Pennyman'll whip you senseless."

Mr. Templeton considered this last speech for a moment. "The fool don't know what he bought," he said quietly.

"That's his own business, not yer's. Supper's ready, such as it is." Gump Hoss reached for bowls he had set on the ground near the now steaming pot. "Here ya go, Miss. It ain't the fare you're likely used to, but it's hot and will fill the empty spaces."

"Thank you," I said quietly, reaching for the bowl and spoon he offered.

While we ate the flavorful stew, I considered whether I should pose the queries I harbored. *Where are we going? How much farther do we have to travel? Where is Mr. Pennyman? Why did he not meet the ship? Why didn't we stay the night in the town? When will we be married? What is* Gehenna*?*

Gehenna. The very word engendered evil. I did not know what Gehenna meant in Texas, but I knew the name. In one of The Reverend John Wentworth's spirited sermons, he said that Gehenna had been a city outside of Jerusalem. King Josiah of Judah had gone to war and destroyed it because Gehenna was a place where human sacrifices were made to Molech, a pagan god.

No, I would hold my questions for now. The Butternut Man was not disposed to civil conversation. I had met only one man more detestable than Percival Templeton. And that man's fate was unknown to me.

I handed the spoon and empty bowl back to Gump Hoss and offered to help him clean up after the meal.

"I doubt yeh've ever washed a dish in yer life," Mr.

Templeton snorted.

"That's not necessary, Miss. There ain't much to do. We'll be getting up early in the morning. Why don't you turn in?" Gump Hoss said, glaring at the younger man.

"Where am I to sleep?" I enquired.

"On that blanket, where I can keep an eye on yeh," Templeton spat.

I recoiled in horror at the idea of having to sleep so near the soldier, much less bring myself to think about whatever lived in this desolate land creeping about in the dark and across my person.

"I made up a pallet for yeh up in the wagon, Miss. You'll be more comfortable off'n the ground," Gump Hoss said. "Off with yeh, now."

"Thank you," I was grateful to the older man for his kindness. I made myself look at Mr. Templeton. "I hope you both pass a pleasant night."

The former Confederate grunted in reply and rolled onto his back.

After removing my dress, crinoline, and corset, I had lain on the blanket-covered straw, wrapped in my shawl, and fallen asleep almost immediately. I awoke before daylight from a terrible dream remembered only in fragments. I sat up and peeked over the edge of the wagon. The silhouetted form of Mr. Templeton lay on his side by the glowing embers of the banked fire. His head was pillowed on one arm. I did not see Gump Hoss, which disturbed me.

I carefully climbed down from the wagon bed and headed for the boulder. Dressed only in my cotton chemise, I found the air warmer than I had anticipated, though I pulled my shawl tightly around myself.

“You be careful walking through them trees,” a voice whispered. I jumped at the interruption of the quiet.

Realizing the voice belonged to Gump Hoss, I looked around, though I did not see him. “I will,” I whispered back.

The sky had begun to lighten as I came back to the wagon. Gump Hoss was building up the fire.

I groped about in the wagon bed and located the clothing I had discarded the night before. I dressed, using the conveyance as a screen.

Mr. Templeton was awake when I came around the wagon and made my way toward the campfire. I sat on a blanket and watched Gump Hoss fry bacon while the sky turned pink.

We each kept our own counsel as breakfast was consumed, and Gump Hoss cleaned up, reloaded the wagon, and harnessed the horses. Mr. Templeton watched but never lent a hand.

The first rays of sunlight extended their tendrils over the horizon of the flat countryside as Gump Hoss guided the horses back onto the track.

The deep brim of my traveling bonnet was not sufficient to keep the sun from its attempts to caress my face. I had not thought to attach a veil, which would have afforded some protection. In desperation, I opened my parasol against the sun’s assault but found the turns in the road limited the parasol’s usefulness. My only recourse was to constantly reposition myself, keeping the skin-ravaging orb at my back.

The unchanging scenery was monotonous. The animals that made their homes in this desolate land did not show themselves. There were no buildings or other signs of people. Maintaining his curmudgeonly behavior, Templeton bemoaned loudly on various topics, then dropped into sullenness.

The sun was close to being directly overhead when the wagon made another detour from the rutted path and stopped. Gump Hoss disconnected the horses from the wagon. Fastening a weighted lead to each of their halters, he led them to a stream. Dropping the weight to the ground, he made sure the reins and chains were slung well over the horses' backs before returning to the wagon.

I found it quite simple to lower the tailgate and extract myself from the wagon without assistance. I set my sights on a large bush and walked purposefully toward it.

"Yeh mind where yeh step, Miss," Gump Hoss warned. "There are critters yeh ought not come in contact with hereabouts."

The advice was disturbing, but I was glad of the caution. As I settled myself to do what needed to be done, I became aware of something hard scraping against my exposed posterior. I screamed and jumped away from the bush. I twirled about, and my skirts fell into place, just in time to see the last of a queer-looking tail disappear beneath the bush.

Gump Hoss came running over, shouting unintelligibly.

"I am fine, Gump Hoss. An animal startled me, but I am uninjured." I called to him.

He stopped on the other side of the bush. "Gracious, Miss. Yeh gave me a fright. What caused yeh to howl?"

"I have not any idea. I saw only its backside as it crawled under the bush. The tail of the beast seemed to be clad in armor."

"Ah, an armadilla. I don't imagine yeh have 'em where yeh come from."

I rounded the bush and came to where Gump Hoss had stopped near the wagon.

"Yeh gotta be mindful of yer surroundings in these parts, Miss. It wouldn't due for yeh to get yersef bit by a Coral

Snake," the older man said with genuine concern. "I don't wanna be the one to tell Mr. Pennyman yeh died of snakebite."

That last bit of information unnerved me. I had never been particularly squeamish about walking in the woods at *Riverbend*. Poisonous snakes were not within my ken. "I shall be more cautious," I assured him.

We returned to the wagon. Mr. Templeton stood, looking out over the small stream, seemingly oblivious to the commotion having occurred at his back. Ignoring him, Gump Hoss rooted about in boxes at the wagon's tail, pulling out cold meat, warm bottles, and tin plates.

As we ate, we shared the meager shade of the underdeveloped trees growing at the edge of the stream with the horses. Templeton shifted his gaze from the plain to glower at Gump Hoss and me.

"What's stuck in yer craw?" Gump Hoss enquired, a look of disgust on his face.

"We're still a ways from Gehenna. I don't mean to be on Mr. Pennyman's bad side by draggin' in after dark. He ain't gonna cotton to our lollygaggin'." Mr. Templeton spat the words as though they burned his mouth

"He'd be a sight more angry if we come in with a lame horse. They needed water and restin'. So did Miss Llewellyn. She should be ridin' in a fine carriage, not the bed of a farm wagon like a serving girl. I ain't seen you settin' up on that box since we stopped. You jumped down afore the wheels stopped turnin'. We will git to Gehenna afore dark," the older man said, not meeting Templeton's eyes. He watched the horses cropping the sparse vegetation under the trees.

"The horses are rested. So're we. Let's get goin'." Templeton looked at me as he thrust the plate at Gump Hoss and took the few steps to the wagon.

“We’d get goin’ faster if’n you’d help hitch the horses,” Gump Hoss pointed out.

“Ain’t my job,” the younger man replied and stayed where he sat.

“I will help you,” I offered. “My father bred and trained horses. I know how to hold them.”

“Ye’ll spoil yer dress.” Gump Hoss said, shaking his head.

“It is already soiled. I do not mind helping, really.” I took hold of the halter of one of the horses while Gump Hoss led the other to the wagon and began attaching the chains.

Chapter 10

The rhythmic noises of the wagon conspired with the warmth of the sun. I was soon asleep.

I woke at dusk as Gump Hoss guided the conveyance into a sweeping left turn and started up a tree-lined lane rife with ruts and potholes. A weathered wooden arch announced our arrival at Gehenna in crudely carved letters about a half-mile down this tortuous path. We passed under the arch and traveled a few hundred feet further where the track forked. The teamster guided the horses to the right to circle a failing flower garden, calling the team to a halt in front of the house.

The Federalist-style house was three stories. A flight of wide steps terminated at a broad, covered porch, with mismatched chairs and low tables scattered haphazardly about, giving an impression of untidiness.

Mr. Templeton was talking and gesturing to Gump Hoss, expressing displeasure that the wagon had not been driven directly to the back of the house. Gump Hoss ignored him, jumped from the driver's seat, and came around to assist my dismount from the wagon.

As I settled my dress, smoothed my hair, and straightened my bonnet, Gump Hoss nodded his approval, regained his seat, and took up the reins. The door of the house opened. A short, plump woman wearing a plain black dress with a white collar and cuffs stepped onto the porch. A starched white day cap partially concealed perfectly coiffed graying hair. She stopped at the top step, hands folded neatly at her waist. Her silver chatelaine caught the last rays of the setting sun.

I started up the steps, hoping circulation would return to

my lower limbs.

“Good evening, Miss Llewellyn. Welcome to Gehenna. I’m Mrs. Hudson, Mr. Pennyman’s housekeeper. The master has not yet come in from the pastures. You have time to tidy yourself before he’s expected.” Her face remained expressionless as she took in my appearance.

I heard the wagon move away and saw it disappear around the corner of the house. My stomach made a hideous sound I hoped had not been heard by any but myself. The grit from traveling on dirt roads clung to my face and clothing.

“I must look a sight,” I said as we crossed the threshold into the foyer.

“I’ll show you to your room.” Mrs. Hudson hastened me through the spacious foyer and up a curving staircase to the second floor. We walked down a long hall with closed doors on either side. She opened the last door on the right to reveal a sparsely furnished room of doubtful color. The window was open to the light evening breeze. The heavy draperies did not move.

“This is to be your room,” Mrs. Hudson said with a dour look.

“Thank you, Mrs. Hudson.”

“I will send Elizabeth up straight away. She’s the housemaid but will also perform the duties of your lady’s maid.”

“Thank you,” I repeated as I removed gloves and bonnet and dropped them on the narrow bed. “I can manage until she comes up.”

Mrs. Hudson held her place for a moment as though in thought. With a sigh, she started to leave, stopped, turned, and opened her mouth. Apparently thinking better of it, she left the room, quietly shutting the door behind her.

I turned around in place, taking careful inventory of the room. The furnishings and décor were of poorer quality than what I had glimpsed in the foyer. The walls were haphazardly whitewashed, with streaks, gaps, and clumps in the brushstrokes. Patches of bare plaster were testament to the workman's haste in completing his task. Heavy lace curtains hidden behind faded velvet draperies allowed little sunlight into the room. The furniture was mismatched. No adornments graced the walls.

A threadbare, once-red counterpane was thrown carelessly over the bare ticked mattress on the black iron bed. The chair appeared to be cherry. The oak wardrobe was stained very dark, almost black.

A cracked mirror had been affixed to the exterior of one wardrobe door. A small, once-white table sat on uneven legs beside the narrow bed. A shallow, dished holder gripped the stub of a lone, nearly guttered candlestick and precariously clung to the tilting table. I noticed there was no washstand.

A soft knock at the door preceded a woman about my age. With toweling tucked under one arm, she carried a bowl and ewer in both hands. I wondered how she had opened the door. She glanced about the room and set the washbasin and pitcher on the chair.

She looked at me with soft brown eyes. "Good evening, Miss. I reckon you'll want to wash and change out of your traveling clothes. It might be some time before your baggage is brought into the house."

"That would be lovely. I have been wearing these clothes since early yesterday morning."

"I will come back to help you dress after your baggage has been brought up."

"Thank you. Elizabeth, is it?"

"Yes, Miss." She left as quietly as she arrived.

I moved my bonnet and gloves to the lopsided table and lay on the bed, glad for some time to myself.

Josiah Pennyman stood at the bottom of the stairs. His well-tailored linen suit, white shirt, and dark blue tie accentuated his deeply tanned face and hands. His eyes followed my progress down the stairs.

Washing away the grit and grime of travel, combined with a brief nap on a real bed, had revived me. I wore the burgundy silk dinner dress. Elizabeth had redressed my hair. I felt refreshed and elegant.

As I reached the last step, he bowed deeply, gently took the fingers of my left hand in his right, and brushed his lips lightly across the back of my gloved hand. I tilted my head ever so slightly but remained mute.

“Miss Llewellyn, it is indeed good to know you at long last,” he intoned.

“I am pleased to make your acquaintance, Mr. Pennyman.” His dark hair was pomaded and parted on the left. His brown eyes were difficult to read. They may have been kindly but had a hard edge to them that gave warning to quick judgment of his character.

We remained in that pose for some moments, gathering our first impressions of the other. His scrutiny was becoming uncomfortable. I looked over his shoulder toward the opposite side of the foyer, wondering what rooms lay beyond the closed doors.

He recovered from his reverie, dropped my hand, and stepped aside that I might quit the final step. With four long strides, he crossed the hallway, stopping at the door furthest from the outside entrance. He made a shallow bow, indicating that I should enter.

Cream-colored walls, light lace curtains under brocade draperies, the dark mahogany table, chairs, and sideboard combined to present an elegant dining room. Paintings of California gold miners and pastoral meadows in beautifully carved frames graced the walls with simplicity. A large crystal chandelier hung over the table but did not dominate the room.

There were eight chairs around the table. Twelve additional chairs stood like soldiers against the walls. The table was set for two.

We were seated at the table before either of us spoke again. "I trust your voyage was not terribly distressing, Miss Llewellyn," Mr. Pennyman ventured.

"The voyage was memorable," I stated, not wishing to regale him with tales of the journey.

"Your father made quite a case for utilizing any other means of travel. I assured him that was the swiftest and safest mode."

Certain that he was enquiring about the voyage out of politeness and not genuine interest, I steered the conversation toward him. "How large is your estate?"

"Gehenna is a cattle ranch, not an estate. It is comprised of some five thousand acres."

Mr. Templeton entered, still wearing his Confederate uniform, followed by a disheveled, nervous-looking, dark-skinned girl wearing an ill-fitting black dress and soiled apron. Neither spoke until the meal had been served and the door closed behind the two servants.

"I was led to believe Mr. Templeton was your agent," I stated.

"I find him useful for certain errands."

"Why does he continue to wear his uniform? General Lee surrendered over a year ago."

He considered this as he raised a crystal wine glass to his lips. "You may have noticed President Johnson's army still infests Corpus Christi. The precious Union has determined that the good people of Texas continue to be a threat to the national welfare. General Lee may have been forced to retire from the field of battle, but the conflict will not be concluded until those Yankee scum vacate the city and allow the citizens of Corpus Christi to govern themselves, as is their right." His voice was cold and vicious.

I felt a chill. I had no doubt he would not hesitate to do violence to anyone contradicting him. I prudently redirected the conversation. "What is it you do with your cattle?"

"I sell them for profit." He warmed to his subject, sitting well back in his chair, holding the glass of wine, and set his gaze on the chandelier. "The cattle are being rounded up now. They scatter all over when they're grazing and calving. We'll sort them and brand the new ones as soon as they're all gathered in one place. I'll cut five hundred head to drive to the New Mexico territory."

"Sort the cattle? Why would you injure your livestock by cutting them? I do not understand." I found myself drawn in by the descriptions of the tasks before him.

"There are few fences in Texas. Cattle from neighboring herds get mixed all together. We sort them out by a mark burned into their hides called a brand. Each ranch has its own brand," he explained. "I'll claim all unbranded heads found on my property unless they're suckling from one of my neighbor's cows. Cutting doesn't mean actually taking a blade to them. It's a means of separating some from the main herd."

"You said something about driving cattle to the New Mexico territory. Is that the same as herding them to market?"

"In a sense. It's the way a large number of cattle are moved long distances."

"Is it a very long distance?"

"About seven hundred miles, give or take."

I could not fathom traveling that distance with five hundred of anything on four legs. "When will you be leaving?"

"Around the first of June. If the weather holds and we don't run into any trouble, we should get them to Fort Sumner before the end of July.

"Our wedding will take place the middle of August."

I was taken aback by the announcement, so casually spoken in conjunction with the timetable for the cattle drive. All thoughts of cattle were driven from my consciousness in favor of this bold statement. My countenance must have registered the surprise of his utterance.

"Miss Llewellyn, are you unwell? Shall I call Mrs. Hudson to assist you?" His face registered concern as he looked at me, a forkful of meat suspended between plate and mouth.

I collected myself sufficiently to speak. "I am fine, Mr. Pennyman. I was so engrossed in your talk of the cattle drive that your pronouncement of our impending marriage took me unawares."

"I beg your pardon. It was not my intention to speak casually of our nuptials." The crease between his eyes seemed to deepen. "I shall be occupied with the round-up and preparations for the drive these coming weeks. It is unfortunate that there will be no time for even the smallest ceremony until after my return."

"I have lived on a farm the whole of my life. I understand the urgency of reaping crops and taking livestock to market. Though I must admit, our people did not move more than two dozen animals at a time, and never the distances you speak of. The prospect of convincing five hundred beasts to travel such a distance is rather outside my ken."

"Yes. Quite." Mr. Pennyman seemed to be juggling many thoughts. He sat in contemplation for some minutes, absently refilling his wine glass. "I shall be sorry to leave you so soon after your arrival. I suspect you and Mrs. Hudson will have much to discuss. She's been my housekeeper since this house was built. She established the household." He stopped long enough to take another mouthful of beef and a healthy swallow of wine, not savoring either. "Mrs. Hudson will show you the house and introduce you to the staff." He paused a moment. "You'll not have a lady's maid."

"I managed the whole of the journey without one. It will be of little inconvenience." I smiled in spite of myself. His statement, said with such conviction, amused me. Mr. Pennyman was obviously unknowledgeable of the arrangement Mrs. Hudson had made with Elizabeth.

The conversation lapsed, and we ate in silence.

He finished his meal, wiped his mouth on a napkin, and stood. "I will leave you to get settled," he shot over his shoulder as he opened the door. "Good night."

"Good night," I replied to the already closed door.

I left the dining room and returned to my bedchamber. Elizabeth looked up from the dress she had been inspecting when I opened the door. "I thought I'd be finished unpacking your things before you retired, Miss."

"Events of the evening took an unexpected turn." My voice was flat, reflecting disappointment that Mr. Pennyman's priorities lay in a different direction than mine. I squeezed between a trunk and the bed to settle in the chair.

I idly pleated and smoothed the fabric of my skirt while watching the housemaid remove items from the trunk, inspect them, and decide where they should reside. There was a pile of clothing on the bed. Recognizing the fabrics, I knew they were destined for the laundry tub.

Elizabeth disappeared behind the bed. She made a noise and rose, unfurling a piece of white cotton. Almost reverently, she placed it on the bed and folded the rent garment so that the frayed edges of the ruined chemise lay close together.

"What in heaven's name happened to this?" Elizabeth breathed.

Visions of Crenshaw swam to the surface of my mind. A shiver coursed through my being at the recollection of that stormy morning. I stood on wobbly limbs and turned toward the window, working to push the dark memories to the inner recesses of my mind, where they may be laid to rest once more. "Destroy it." The harshness in my voice startled both of us. I had not meant the words to carry the raw emotion they so obviously did. "It is beyond repair," I said in a more subtle tone, looking down at my hands.

"Yes, Miss. Of course." Elizabeth glanced at me with curiosity and sympathy but turned back to the trunk, working silently and efficiently. "Are you cold, Miss? Do you want a shawl?"

"No, thank you, Elizabeth. Someone just walked across my grave." My back was to her. I was glad for the heavy drapery at the window that did not allow for reflection in the glass. Gaining my composure, I turned and sat again. I wanted a diversion to keep the demons in their place. "How long have you been in Mr. Pennyman's employ?" I asked.

"Six months," she replied. Elizabeth's speech lacked the accent that marked people of the Southern states. While not trained in linguistics, I was familiar with some of the peculiarities of speech in the northern states and thought her people might hail from the environs of Pennsylvania.

"Have you been in Texas long?"

"No, Miss. About nine months." Her work finished, Elizabeth closed the trunk and pulled it into the hallway to join its companion. "Templeton or Jenkins will put your trunks in the attic," she informed me as she gathered the clothing on the bed. "Are you ready to retire? I can come back to assist you."

"No, I think I'll sit up for a while longer. I can manage. Thank you, Elizabeth. You need not return tonight." I wanted to be alone to think about the conversation at supper. June was but a few weeks away. Mr. Pennyman and I would have little time to become acquainted before he left.

The housemaid turned as she started out the door. "Good night, Miss," she said, smiling as she shut the door.

I do not know how long I sat in contemplation. I was aware of hearing a door close and thought it must be Mr. Pennyman retiring. The candle had been replaced earlier in the evening. It was now sputtering and quite near guttering. I opened the drawer in the tilting table. Two new candles and a box of lucifers lay within. I picked up one of the candles, lit it with the flickering stub, and held the other end over the failing flame before seating the new light with a faint squish on top of the soft beeswax in the candleholder.

I changed into my nightdress, anticipating the gentle comforts of a feather bed. Sheets had been put on the mattress while I was at supper. I luxuriated in the feel of the clean cotton sheets and the softness of the mattress beneath me. The scents of lye soap and lavender engulfed my senses. The small clock on the bedside table ticked comfortingly in the silence of the night. I extinguished the candle, rolled onto my side, and drifted into a deep and dreamless sleep.

Chapter 11

The remains of a breakfast sat at the place Mr. Pennyman had occupied the previous night. He was not in the room, and I surmised I had missed seeing him by very little time. Sitting alone, enjoying eggs and tea, I wondered how I would productively fill my days. There were no other women save the servants. Without the responsibilities of mistress of the house, I was as much adrift on land as I had been while on the sea. Speculation regarding my life in this house as Josiah Pennyman's betrothed was interrupted by Mrs. Hudson.

"Good morning, Miss," the housekeeper began. "I trust you passed a restful night."

"Good morning, Mrs. Hudson. It was lovely to sleep in a real bed. Thank you for inquiring."

"Mr. Pennyman has instructed me to show you about."

"Yes, he said as much last night. I have finished breaking my fast."

"Shall we start, then?"

"Yes, please."

My tour began in the foyer. We looked in the parlor and library. The rooms on the first floor were beautifully and expensively decorated. Silk wall coverings, brocaded draperies, lace under curtains, and Chippendale and Hepplewhite furniture graced each room.

Mrs. Hudson started up the stairs. I stopped and opened the only door we had not peered around. As I stepped over the threshold, I knew this to be Josiah Pennyman's study. The room was paneled with dark wood. A large leather chair sat behind an immense desk. Two straight-backed wooden chairs stood ready to receive visitors.

"Miss Llewellyn," Mrs. Hudson's disapproving tone startled me. "How did you gain entrance to this room?"

"The door was unlocked."

"It would not bode well if Mr. Pennyman was to find you in there. That door is kept locked, and he has the only key." She carefully stayed outside the room, frequently looking over her shoulders and wringing her hands in agitation. "If the door is unlocked, he is nearby. Quickly, we must get upstairs before he sees you in there." The urgency in her voice animated my feet. Shutting the door, we climbed the stairs, our footfalls slowing as we approached the second floor.

"All of the bedchambers are on this level." Mrs. Hudson explained as we stopped at the first door on the left. "This is Mr. Pennyman's chamber."

After her reaction to my entering the study, I was surprised when she opened the door to show me this room. But then, I realized she likely assumed I would soon be sharing it. I felt myself blush as I poked my head in while taking pains to stay in the hallway.

This room had been decorated with the same elegance as the first-floor rooms. The bedclothes, drapery fabrics, and furniture style showed an apparent masculine influence.

Quietly closing the door, we moved down the hallway toward the back staircase used by the staff.

"What about the other bedchambers?" I asked.

"There is nothing to show you." Mrs. Hudson's reply carried a note of regret.

"I do not understand."

"Save the chamber you occupy, none have been finished."

In disbelief, I opened a door to find she spoke the truth. The walls were bare lathe. A thick layer of dust lay on the floors. Cobwebs hung from the high ceiling. Heavy and worn draperies hung at the window, thrusting the room into inky darkness.

"Why have these rooms not been completed?" I asked.

"That is a question for Mr. Pennyman, Miss."

We returned to our original route and went to the third floor. "These are the servant quarters. Not all of them are occupied. This is one of the unoccupied rooms. They're all the same." She opened one of the doors.

The small room was furnished with beds, dressers, and writing tables for two occupants. The walls were white. Muslin curtains hung at the closed window. Bare mattresses were folded over on themselves, exposing half of the otherwise hidden parts of the bed frames. A thin layer of dust lay on the floor and furniture.

"Have all the unused rooms on this floor been finished?" I asked.

"Yes. Though, I don't know why."

We backed out of the room, closing the door behind us. The hallway ended at the staircase that wound down three flights, with landings and doors leading to the second and first floors before ending in the servants' common room. A long, sturdy table with mismatched chairs all around was the dominant feature of this room. A large window spanned nearly an entire wall, with a view of the courtyard beyond. Doors in the other three walls led to other parts of the service level.

I followed Mrs. Hudson as she skirted the table and stopped next to her in a long, wide hallway. One end terminated at a door, which was open. A light breeze wafted through, fluttering the hem of my skirt. The other end concluded in a staircase leading to a butler's pantry adjoining the dining room.

Mrs. Hudson clapped her hands twice. The house staff quietly gathered in the hall and formed a line.

"You are acquainted with Mr. Templeton." Mrs. Hudson left no room for comment. Still dressed in the Confederate uniform, his face was set in a sinister sneer.

Indicating the thin woman standing next to the former soldier, she continued her introductions, "Mrs. O'Malley is Mr. Pennyman's cook. She's been with him since he came to Texas. You've also met Elizabeth."

I recognized the last girl as the one who had helped serve supper. "Amparo is our kitchen maid." She continued, "This lady is Miss Llewellyn. Thank you. You may return to your duties."

The little group moved in different directions. I fell in step with Mrs. Hudson, up the stairs, through the small room, and into the foyer.

"Why is Mr. Templeton included in the house staff?" I was curious what role he played in the household.

"He claims to be the butler." Her disapproving tone and the grim look on her face told me to ask no more about the Butternut Man.

"We are given to understand you are to be mistress of this ranch," Mrs. Hudson said.

Unaccustomed to such forwardness in a servant, I was taken aback and took a moment before responding. "I am under the same impression."

The older woman failed to mask her face well. A look of disapproval briefly crossed it. She selected the pocket watch from several items dangling from the chatelaine affixed to the waistband of her dress. Consulting the timepiece, she exclaimed, "Dear me, I had no idea of the hour. Please, excuse me."

As she bustled toward the stairs, I asked, "One more thing. Does Mr. Pennyman ordinarily dress for supper?"

She twisted her body toward me, her brow furrowed as she processed the query. "Why, no. He is in the habit of taking a light supper in his study."

"Oh, dear." I was at a loss as to how to continue this conversation.

"Mr. Pennyman rings when he is ready for it." A pensive expression was fixed on Mrs. Hudson's face. "He works late into the night."

"Thank you, Mrs. Hudson."

She left to resume her work. I turned toward the library in search of something new to read.

The library at Gehenna was easily twice the size of the library at Riverbend. I had never seen so many books in a single room. Three walls were covered floor to ceiling by shelves filled with leather and cloth-bound volumes. Double French doors opened onto the dooryard and were centered on the fourth wall, with bookcases on either side and above.

The room was furnished with a large over-stuffed horsehair divan, a pair of burgundy leather wing chairs, and a rectangular table with eight Windsor chairs tucked around it. Overwhelmed by the number of books, I decided logic dictated starting to the left of the door opening from the foyer.

Locating the ladder, I brought it around and climbed to the top shelf. The absence of dust on the upper shelves and books was a tribute to Mrs. Hudson and Elizabeth. Pulling a book from the shelf, I found it to be *House of the Seven Gables* by Nathaniel Hawthorne. Having never read it, I brought it down with me.

I had intended to take it to my room to read but thought better of that idea. There was no reason to sequester myself in that dreary chamber when I could remain in this large, comfortable room. Making myself comfortable on the divan, I opened the book and began to read.

I was deep into the story when Mrs. Hudson announced the mid-day meal.

After dining alone, I retrieved my writing box and returned to the library. I wrote in my journal, penned letters to Melissa Brandt and Rachel Downs, my friends in Norwich, and then resumed reading.

Tea was served promptly at 4:00 p.m. in the library at my request. I sat at the table, ate warm biscuits dripping with butter, drank the strong, hot tea, and continued reading.

I was remotely aware of the tall clock chiming six. Lost in contemplation on the decadence of idleness, I did not hear Mr. Pennyman come in. He discreetly cleared his throat and settled into one of the wing chairs. I looked about, orienting myself to place and time.

"I trust you've had a relaxing day," he said, a small smile playing on his mouth.

"Yes, I have. It seems queer to be completely still after so many days in constant motion. The ship was never at rest, always moving, even in port. I had no time to become accustomed to walking on land before being installed in the bed of your wagon."

"You sat in the wagon bed? With the supplies?" He was visibly distressed to learn this. "Who rode in the carriage?"

"There was no carriage, just the wagon. Gump Hoss and Mr. Templeton sat on the teamster's box." I pondered whether I should convey the coarse treatment I received at his agent's hands.

The question was moot. Mr. Pennyman was at the bellpull in two steps, expectantly facing the door.

After a brief wait, Mrs. Hudson came into the room.

"Where is Templeton?" Mr. Pennyman demanded.

"I do not know," Mrs. Hudson responded, standing a bit straighter.

"Find him."

"I have not seen him since I introduced the house staff to Miss Llewellyn this morning. Where do you suggest I look?" She neither cowered nor averted her gaze from her employer.

I sat mutely throughout this conversation, transfixed by the temerity of the housekeeper to speak so boldly to her employer.

His posture relaxed slightly, but he remained standing. "Did he say anything about what he would be doing today?"

"No, sir. Mr. Templeton does not confide in me."

"Or anyone else," he said under his breath. With increased volume, he instructed, "Have Jenkins look in his room and the outbuildings and make inquiries in the bunkhouse."

"Yes, sir." Mrs. Hudson started to back out of the room but was stopped as Mr. Pennyman gave one more instruction.

Pointing at the tea tray, his face once again clouding, he commanded, "Remove this tray."

Mrs. Hudson scurried forward, picked up the tray with practiced precision, and left the library.

Percival Templeton seemed to have vanished from Gehenna, though his method of removal remained unknown. None of the horses appeared to be missing. No visitors had been seen on the property.

The search was called off at nightfall, to be resumed at first light, should he not have returned.

Mr. Pennyman's disposition deteriorated with each passing hour. He vacillated between raving vulgarities and quiet seething.

My emotional state was contradictory. I was remorseful that my comments about the wagon ride had thrown the entire household into turmoil. But I was pleased that Mr. Templeton was to be called to answer for my rough treatment during the time he was charged with my safety.

After a supper of cold beef and greens, Mr. Pennyman retired to his study. I retreated to the library. Having left the door standing open, I was privy to the parade of people summoned to the study to aid in the reconstruction of Templeton's day and, quite possibly, provide some clue to his whereabouts.

Around ten o'clock, I gave up the vigil and retired for the night.

The stars were still shining brightly when I was awakened by shouting and unidentifiable loud noises in the dooryard. Tossing back the bedclothes, I went to the window to investigate the commotion.

The moon had set. I heard voices but could not discern what the men were saying. One voice was recognizable. His Southern tenor, even slurred by strong drink, was distinctive.

I stood in the dark and looked out the window into the black night, wondering whether they had awakened anyone else. It would be easy to alert the household, but I saw no purpose in it. The men in the dooryard seemed to be of no danger to anyone save themselves.

The sudden cessation of their clamor gave me pause to believe the men had lapsed into unconsciousness. I was on the verge of returning to my bed when the clink of steel striking a flint carried up to me in the quiet night. As my eyes and ears strained to locate the source, the scent of smoke filled my nose, and I saw a slender flame reaching for fuel to continue its life in the dry circular garden.

As I reached for the bell pull, a rose bush burst into flames, illuminating the yard and four men in butternut uniforms gaping at their handiwork.

Mrs. Hudson and Elizabeth rushed into my room as the flames began to fold into themselves, and another bush ignited, sparks spraying the garden as heated sap exploded.

I heard Mrs. Hudson pounding on Mr. Pennyman's chamber door, shouting that the garden was on fire. Elizabeth took in the scene below and fled the room. I heard her bounding down the back stairs.

I was rooted to the spot in front of the window, transfixed by the four men in the dooryard. Mr. Templeton threw his head back and shouted something unintelligible through the hissing and spitting fire. It seemed to animate his companions, who began shouting and dancing about, seemingly pleased with the results of their antics.

I do not know when Mrs. Hudson returned to my room. I became aware that she had somehow gotten me into my dressing gown and was tying the sash. At the same time, she was encouraging me to fit my feet into house slippers while pulling me toward the door.

A bell was tolling from somewhere, and more voices joined the quartet below. Mrs. Hudson and I took the back stairs to the service level and out the back door. She settled me on a bench in the gazebo with an admonition to stay there until she came for me.

The cool night air brought me out of myself, and I watched from my secluded spot as the field hands formed a bucket line. I felt useless sitting in the dark while others were frantically working to extinguish the fire.

Elizabeth and Mrs. O'Malley joined me in the gazebo, looking dazed. I do not know whether Mrs. O'Malley was awakened by the bell or Mrs. Hudson. They took no notice of me as they huddled together in the little open-sided building.

Shouts that the fire was extinguished and no more water was required came down the line. The men stopped passing buckets and milled about the courtyard, unsure whether to return to their beds or begin the day's work.

"What in the name of all that's holy happened?" Elizabeth implored, standing and taking a step away from Mrs. O'Malley.

"Mr. Templeton and his friends set fire to the dooryard garden," I reported.

The women turned and looked at me, their expressions indicating they did not know I was sitting so near them. "So, he came back," the cook uttered.

The sky was beginning to lighten. One could make out shadowy shapes milling about, waiting for directions. Mr. Pennyman, his nightshirt stuffed into the front of his trousers but hanging loose in the back, came around the corner of the house. Even in the pre-dawn light, I could see sooty streaks on his face and clothes. He lifted his hands over his head. The men quieted, waiting for their employer to speak.

"The fire is out." Mr. Pennyman put down his arms. "It was confined to the circle garden. None of our people were hurt. You all get cleaned up and break your fast. You know what has to be done today."

Concluding his speech, he headed toward the gazebo. “Why are all of you out here?”

Mrs. O’Malley spoke for all of us, “Mrs. Hudson sent us out here in case the house caught fire.”

“Of course she did,” he responded. “Go back inside and put on some clothes.”

The two women did not hesitate but went directly to the back door of the house. Heeding Mrs. Hudson’s admonishment, I remained where I was.

“Get yourself inside, Miss Llewellyn. These men don’t need to see you in your nightclothes.”

“I was instructed to stay here until Mrs. Hudson came for me. I intend to do so.” I did not want to tell him about the horrible consequences I nearly suffered the last time I did not follow instructions.

“Get in that house, now. I will deal with Mrs. Hudson.” The stern look on his face left no doubt that disobeying him at this moment would be at my peril. I rose from the bench and followed the servants into the house. I was nearly to the door when Mr. Pennyman called to me.

“Priscilla, keep your curtains closed, and do not look outside. Once you’re dressed, use the back stairs, take your breakfast in the servants’ common room, and stay there.”

I started to protest that I could not take a meal in the servant’s quarters, but he stopped me. “What happened outside is none of your concern. I’m sorry that you had to witness as much as you did. I will tell you when you may go upstairs.”

Not understanding why I was being sequestered and still somewhat in shock by what I had seen in the garden, I nodded and said, “Yes, of course...Josiah.”

Mrs. Hudson installed me in her sitting room. The door had been left open to allow the cool morning air to drift in. There was an acrid odor that I could not place. I supposed it was something that had burned in the fire. I paced the compact room like one of the caged animals I had seen at a circus when I was a child.

I made every effort not to speculate on what had transpired in the dooryard. I assured myself Josiah would tell me after he dealt with the four men. While I was curious about the whereabouts of Mr. Templeton and his companions, I could not bring myself to contemplate their evil deeds since I last saw Gehenna's butler.

I was not the only person to be confined to the servants' quarters. Elizabeth and Mrs. Hudson were also commanded to remain downstairs until otherwise instructed. This left Elizabeth with little to do. The housemaid's duties were performed in the family and public areas, not in the servant's quarters. She sat at the long table in the common room, her folded hands resting on the tabletop. Although her back was to me, I could see by the set of her back and shoulders that she was deep in thought.

Mrs. Hudson roamed from room to room, picking up candlesticks, salt cellars, bric-a-brac, and putting them back where she found them. Her countenance was that of a person puzzling over a problem. The set of her face changed as she abruptly stopped in front of the room Mr. Templeton had gone to at the conclusion of my tour yesterday morning. Squaring her shoulders, she entered the small room. She sat at the desk and began looking through stacks of papers and opening ledgers.

Mrs. O'Malley was the only one able to go about her ordinary duties. The sounds and fragrances emanating from the kitchen were proof that meal preparation was progressing at a goodly pace.

I was taken aback when I saw Amparo enter the common room with plates and silverware. *Where had she been when we were all out at the gazebo? When had she come downstairs?* Pushing these thoughts aside, I sat in the wing-backed chair and opened the book I'd brought.

The four servants sat at the table with the remains of their morning meal between them. It had been a solemn repast. They talked in hushed tones as they lingered over their morning tea and coffee. I longed to be included in the conversation but knew my place and remained in the housekeeper's sitting room. I could not discern their words, but the resonance of their voices was soothing. I sat in the rocking chair and felt the tension within me diminish.

Time moved slowly as we waited for Josiah to come downstairs or ring for Mrs. Hudson. Mrs. O'Malley and Amparo returned to the kitchen and scullery. Elizabeth followed but soon returned to the common room.

The bell from the study finally rang as Mrs. Hudson's mantel clock chimed nine. The housekeeper rushed up the stairs. The strain of waiting for her return was even more unbearable. I stood at the doorway of the sitting room, willing her to come back downstairs.

She appeared at the foot of the stairs just as suddenly as she had left. She held the banister and wall to steady herself and called Mrs. O'Malley and Amparo to the common room. "You should hear this, too, Miss Llewellyn," Mrs. Hudson said, beckoning me into the room. Her voice quavered strangely, and her face was ashen.

"Garrett Wilkes is dead. Mr. Templeton has been dismissed." Her voice was strong, without waver, but she spoke quietly. The older woman's hands absently played with the objects hanging from her chatelaine. "Thomas Wakefield and Jackson Dummermuth were with them.

"Mr. Pennyman did not inform me what they were about. But, it was no good, for certain and for sure. Any one of them isn't to be trusted further than your arm. Together, they're nothing but trouble.

"Mrs. O'Malley, please prepare a tray for Mr. Pennyman. I'll take it up."

"Ought I add a few morsels for the miscreants?" These were the first words I heard the cook speak. Her voice was deeper than would have been expected for her height, being a woman barely five feet tall. She spoke softly with her eyes trained upon the housekeeper.

"Under other circumstances, I would think it appropriate. Mr. Pennyman is in no mood to be hospitable toward them. No, prepare a tray for one." A note of regret touched Mrs. Hudson's voice. She paused a moment, then gained control of herself. "Elizabeth, you may begin on the bedchambers. Be mindful not to open the draperies in Miss Llewellyn's room. Mr. Pennyman wishes we not view Wilkes' remains."

As the women resumed their duties, Mrs. Hudson turned to me. "Mr. Pennyman said you are to remain here a while longer. He wants to be sure Templeton and his friends are off the property before you return upstairs."

"I see." There was nothing else to say in acknowledgment of this pronouncement. I was mulling over the information she had just imparted. *What mischief had the former*

Confederates been plotting? Dutifully, I returned to the housekeeper's sitting room and waited, albeit not patiently.

Many hours passed before Mr. Pennyman appeared in the doorway of the common room. Elizabeth, having long completed her work in the two occupied bedchambers, now sat at the table replacing a button that had come off a dress and did not hear him on the stairs.

Mrs. Hudson, usually attuned to every movement and noise in the house but now engrossed in documents and ledgers, also did not hear him.

Mrs. O'Malley and Amparo were bustling about the kitchen, chopping, boiling, baking, cooking, and quietly talking, never expecting him to invade their domain.

I was the only person in the servants' quarters to observe his entrance, his forehead creased and mouth pursed as he puzzled through whatever was on his mind.

His footfalls as he entered the common room startled Elizabeth. She emitted a small sound as she pricked her finger with the needle she was pushing through the fabric of the dress. The small noise alerted Mrs. Hudson, her head snapping up as though a cannon had been fired. Even Mrs. O'Malley and Amparo raised their heads in reaction to the softly uttered noise. Mr. Pennyman, also startled out of his reverie, looked upon the young woman with wonderment as though he was orienting himself to his surroundings.

Without an utterance, the women servants discontinued their activities to gather around the table in the common room. I moved to stand behind a chair.

Mr. Pennyman stood at the head of the table. The toll of the morning's events was reflected in the carriage of his form and the lines and creases on his face. He looked around at the feminine faces waiting for his speech and exhaled deeply. The simple act of exchanging breath did nothing to assuage our anxieties.

It seemed as though those few moments were minutes or hours. We watched him, our imaginations drawing pictures of the early morning horror in the dooryard too frightening to translate into speech.

He found his voice, speaking softly, carefully choosing his words. "The miscreants are gone. It seems that setting fire to the garden was an act born of middling whiskey and bad judgment." He stopped speaking, though it was apparent he wanted to say more.

We remained where we were, standing and sitting around the table, watching him struggle with his thoughts.

"You may all go about your business." His shoulders slumped ever so slightly, and he continued to stare at the tabletop, tracing the wood grain with a fingertip.

No one spoke. Mrs. O'Malley and Amparo took a step backward, away from the table, then turned and walked slowly back to the kitchen. Mrs. Hudson returned to the little room and resumed her inspection of the documents and ledgers ordinarily maintained by the butler.

I walked around the table to where Josiah stood and touched the sleeve of his shirt gently, with just my fingertips. He looked up, an unexplainable expression crossing his face until recognition returned.

"Take yourself upstairs, now," he whispered. "I'll be up in a little while. I've some business yet down here." He tentatively touched my cheek, then turned to talk with Mrs. Hudson.

Chapter 12

The remainder of my first week at Gehenna passed quietly. I was given to understand the dead man had family in the area. His shrouded body was put in a wagon and taken to them for burial.

Although no one spoke of Mr. Templeton, he was frequently in my thoughts. I did not need to know him well to know he was not a man to be summarily dismissed. He would want his revenge. I surmised he was somewhere licking his wounds like an injured dog while planning his next move. I decided it was best not to be complacent. He could and would strike when it was least expected. The Butternut Man knew Josiah would be leaving on the cattle drive. The closer that day came, the more wary I became.

There was no time to hire a butler before the cattle drive. The house would be left with no man to protect it. I wondered whether the women had previously been left to their own defense. *Should I ask Mrs. Hudson?*

My household responsibilities were confined to those of a houseguest. I walked in the mornings, acquainting myself with the grounds near the house. There was little to compare to *Riverbend*. This land was devoid of the lush green forest and wide river bordering the Connecticut farm.

The gardens at Gehenna were in a sad state of neglect. The soil was dry and hard. Atrophied bushes languished among sickly weeds. There was scant shade save the small orchard of fruit trees. The ranch sat sufficiently far from the ocean to not benefit from sea breezes. The well stood in the courtyard at the back of the house, but I saw no stream or pond from which crops might be provided water.

The afternoon air was hot and still. I wondered how the people working the fields managed under the blazing, unforgiving sun without respite from their backbreaking work.

I was curious about what was entailed in rounding up cattle. Josiah's efforts to explain the process usually concluded in my collapsing in laughter as he rushed about the library, making strange noises and whirling his arm about his head in imitation of something he called roping. The indignant glare and protestations that his demonstration was not humorous served only to reinforce my mirth.

I spent as little time as possible in the bleak little bedchamber assigned to me. I much preferred the library.

Josiah rose early and worked late into the night. I rarely saw him before supper. After the evening meal, he would spend an hour or so with me before sequestering himself in his study.

It is easy to lose track of days and dates when you have no responsibilities. So it was that Sunday came without my knowledge of the exact day of the week. I was surprised to find Josiah seated at the dining table, pouring over some papers and absently eating his breakfast.

Not wishing to disturb his concentration, I quietly filled my plate from the sideboard and took my place at the table. He looked over the page he was reading and snapped, "Are you in the habit of not acknowledging people when you enter a room?"

"Good morning, Josiah," I replied in a cheery tone. "I trust you passed a restful night." I allowed the greeting to settle before responding to his question. "You appeared engrossed in your reading. I had no desire to interrupt."

He did not respond, nor had he put down the page in his left hand. When it was clear he had no intention of answering, I adopted his tenor.

"You ought not to criticize another's manners when you have no intention of complying with convention." I tried to put a hard edge on the words but did not succeed.

He peered at me over the document in his hand. "I am corrected. What is the old adage? 'Do as I say…?'"

"'Practice what you preach.'" I quoted.

"Ah, yes, that would be the one." He carefully set aside the documents, giving me his full attention. "Did you have something specific you wanted to discuss?"

"No, merely that it is pleasant to share the morning meal with you. Why are you so late leaving the house today?"

"My calendar tells me it is Sunday. The cattle drive will be leaving next week. Preparations have gone well, and I find there is little left to do. I thought we might spend the day together."

"Oh, I would like nothing better."

The conversation continued, stilted and banal. Gradually, we were able to draw each other out and learned we had some common interests.

I allowed myself to begin to believe that life with Josiah Pennyman might be pleasant. I made every effort to ignore the dark looks I had seen, the sharp comments, and his judgment in butlers.

Josiah and I were enjoying a leisurely walk through the orchard when I gathered my courage to say some of what had been troubling me. "What would you have me do while you are away?"

"I have pondered that very question," he responded. He

leaned against a tree trunk and plucked a piece of unripe fruit from a limb near his head. "There is a wedding to plan. And your bedchamber is not well finished. I am surprised you have not spoken of its sad condition." He tossed the strange-looking hard red bulb into the air, deftly catching it.

"It is not my place to comment on the manner in which you choose to finish your home. I am but a guest."

"You are, in fact, more than a guest. In two months, you shall be Mistress of Gehenna. Your chamber should reflect your station. I shall write to my builder, providing a budget for the work. You may do as you will with the room."

In my brief acquaintance with this man, I had not known him to be generous. He was demanding and hard, his temper quick. I knew I should be delighted at the prospect of the project and not question his motive. But, question it, I did.

"Did I say something wrong?" he enquired. The tone of his voice did not encourage expounding upon the subject.

"No. I...I need to think." I continued walking through the orchard, occasionally touching leaves and scrutinizing the unfamiliar fruit.

Josiah stayed behind but eventually followed me, quickly catching up with his long strides and my lazy stroll.

"Are you unhappy here?" he asked.

It was a direct question and deserved a direct answer. "No, but neither am I happy."

"Have you been mistreated?"

How to answer that question? Of course, I had been mistreated by Mr. Templeton. But, since my arrival at Gehenna, I had been treated with kindness and respect.

"No, but neither have I been overwhelmed with kindness. I have passed a solitary existence with little knowledge of the pastimes offered by Gehenna, save your abundant library.

“I hold no animosity, Josiah. I do understand you have been immersed in preparations for your cattle drive. I have been leading a solitary life in the midst of people since I boarded *The Emma* in Boston. I yearn for the society of others.”

“The social life you enjoyed in Connecticut does not, and will not, exist at Gehenna. I have worked hard to build this ranch. Frivolity has no place here. Our nearest neighbor is half a day’s ride. You must content yourself with whatever pleasures you may derive from the land.”

“I understand this, Josiah. However, it is no easy matter to reconcile. I shall spend the weeks you are away becoming accustomed to having no one in whom I may confide or even while away an afternoon.

“How am I to plan a wedding or decorate a room with little means of communication with the world outside Gehenna?”

“Gump Hoss will see that your letters and messages are delivered. He will remain here while I am gone.”

There was a lull in the conversation. I walked further into the orchard. Josiah lagged, inspecting the fruit and trees. I stopped at the outer edge of the orchard and looked at the barren plain beyond. I was struck with the desolation of this place and wondered whether I could ever call it home. I do not believe I had ever felt as alone as I felt at that moment.

Josiah came up to stand beside me. We watched the plain for some little time without words passing between us. He tentatively placed a hand on my shoulder and drew me nearer him.

“I do wish for you to want to be here. What can I do?” he asked.

“There is nothing for you to do. It is a condition I must

achieve on my own. This Texas of yours is not within my ken. I suppose, with time, it will become as familiar to me as Connecticut."

He was quiet momentarily, then asked, "Would it please you to have your father at the wedding?"

I had not anticipated the question. I did not look at Josiah but kept my eyes trained on the open ground before us. "It is my heart's desire."

"I was surprised he did not accompany you. Write to him. Tell him we both want him to be here."

"There is no hope for it. He would not receive the letter in time."

"We can wait for him to arrive. There is no urgency to wed."

"He is occupied with a new venture."

I felt him start. He dropped his arm and asked, "Surely business matters would not keep him away. Does he have an indisposition to traveling? Is he ill?"

"He was quite well when I last saw him. He has embarked on an ocean voyage." I laughed at the allusion to my ill-founded predilection.

I hazarded a glance at the man beside me. The look of surprise on Josiah's face gave me to understand that he knew nothing of Papa's plans to quit the country. "When will he return?"

Cautiously, I responded, "I do not foresee his return. It was his intent to be buried in Africa."

"What business does he have so far from home?"

"After the conclusion of the rebellion, Papa joined the American Colonization Society. He's on one of their ships, delivering Negroes to Liberia."

Gehenna's master roughly took hold of my upper limbs and turned me to face him. "What about his holdings?" he shouted, his face crimson. "Does he have an agent managing his affairs?"

"Papa told me he intended to liquidate his assets before he departed. I have no knowledge of an agent." I tried to keep my voice calm but was alarmed by his reaction. He became more agitated with each answer I provided, shaking me violently.

"What about the farm?" he demanded.

I was reluctant to provide the answer I was certain Josiah did not want to hear. "He sold *Riverbend* to one of our neighbors," I responded in a small voice. Uncertain how he would react to this news, I desperately wanted to get away from this man.

He cast me aside as he released my arms. Unable to maintain my balance, I stumbled and fell into the lane between the trees, the wind forced from my body by the impact. Closing my eyes, I willed myself to resume breathing. When I opened them again, it was to see the retreating form of Josiah Pennyman.

I lay in the orchard, too stunned to move, tears staining my cheeks. After rising, I stayed amongst the trees until the sun started to sink below the horizon. Returning to the yard, I sat in the gazebo, all the while working to make sense of Josiah's reaction to what I had told him.

That Josiah devised to marry me to obtain my father's wealth was incomprehensible. *In what enterprise were Papa and Josiah involved? What, or who was Papa running from? What was Papa concealing with his sudden philanthropic bent toward the Negroes?* I had declined to entertain these questions, burying them in the inner recesses of my mind. I could not fathom my parent involved in war profiteering. It was an absurd notion. Yet, Papa had alluded to that fact last year. I was certain the evidence was somewhere in Josiah's study. I had to know the truth about the business ventures of which Papa spoke the night he told me of my betrothal to the Master of Gehenna.

It was dusk when Elizabeth found me. Without speaking, she guided me into the house and up the stairs to dress for supper.

I was late coming to the dining room. Josiah was already seated when I entered.

"So, you decided to grace us with your presence. Sit yourself down." His voice was deep and harsh.

"I lost track of the time." I remained standing, arguing with myself whether to say what I had practiced while I was dressing.

"Have you ever performed an honest day's work?" he asked.

Why would he ask such a question? "I assure you, Mr. Josiah Pennyman, while I have had certain advantages, I have known a day's work."

"Of course, you have. I'm sure your father had you toiling in the fields before the clout was off your bum. Let me see your hands," he demanded, holding out his calloused hand.

Tentatively, I moved toward him and held out my hands for his inspection. He turned them over. They were the hands of a lady, soft and white.

"How is it you came to know my father?" I asked.

"Business. Your father is a dishonest Yankee snake. He thinks to deprive me of what's rightfully mine by taking it to Africa."

"I know little of Father's affairs. He said you were a business associate but did not elaborate on his enterprises with you. I have no recollection of meeting you or even seeing you at *Riverbend*. What business did you have in New England?"

He laughed as though I had told an amusing story. "You shan't meddle in my affairs. Suffice it to say that your father is playing a dangerous game he will not win. He swindled me out of profits from our venture during the Northern aggression. Now he thinks to deprive me of your inheritance."

I was stunned. "I don't understand. Why are you angry with me? I have done nothing to you."

"You ignorant, penniless, little waif." His tone was hard, and his eyes cruel. "Your benevolent, loving father has left you nothing to inherit." He shook his head and chuckled to himself. "Sit yourself down, or go back to your room."

I fled the room and hurried up the stairs to the dreadful bedchamber, throwing myself across the bed, tears burning my eyes. My last thought as I drifted into unconsciousness was, *Oh, Ethan, why did you have to die?*

Chapter 13

I said not a word to anyone about what had transpired, but I had no doubt the servants knew something was awry. Elizabeth assisted me in dressing for bed, speaking only those words necessary to the task at hand.

I was awake most of the night, pacing the bedchamber, ruminating on the events of the day, my worst fears realized. I climbed into bed and fell asleep as the sun crept over the horizon.

Disturbing dreams of abuse and degradations at the hands of Josiah Pennyman kept the few hours of repose from being restful and restorative. Elizabeth came to wake me. I watched her prepare my morning ablutions.

"Mr. Pennyman wishes to see you before he goes out to the range," she informed me as she removed underpinnings from the wardrobe.

"Good. I have something to say to him, as well." There was a hardness in my speech. "Ask Jenkins to bring down my trunks." The maid looked at me, her eyes wide and mouth slightly open, with an audible intake of breath.

When my morning ablutions were complete, I went downstairs, intent on entering the dining room. I was halfway across the foyer when I heard a door open, and Josiah spoke.

"Priscilla, a few words. Now." His voice was stern but held none of the anger from the previous night.

"Of course," I replied and retraced my steps, entering his study. I began my speech before he had an opportunity to return to his chair.

"It is obvious that your intentions toward me are no longer honorable. I shall leave Gehenna at the earliest convenience. Today, if at all possible. I shall be packed within the hour of my trunks being brought down."

"It is not convenient. I can spare no one to drive you into Corpus Christi. You shall remain here until I have returned from New Mexico."

"And do what?"

His face brightened. Leaning back in his chair, he smiled. "You shall earn your keep by becoming a house servant."

I fell into one of the guest chairs, disbelief writ across my face. "Why would I undertake such an enterprise?"

"As I see it, you have no other option. You have no home, no income, no means of support. You claim you are accustomed to an honest day's work. I mean to offer you that opportunity."

"My financial circumstances are none of your concern." I could feel the heat rising in my face and knew it to be flushed. I stood up, looking at him across his fine, polished desk. "I shall not enter your employ. If you have no one to drive me away from here, please provide me with a horse and carriage. I shall find my own way back to Corpus Christi." I started for the door.

"No."

The single word arrested my steps. I turned to look at him. "Would you keep me here against my will?" Disbelief dripped from my question.

"Yes, if it pleases me, which it does. I cannot allow you to wander about the desert alone. With my butler gone, I am in need of another house servant. You will do nicely. Of course, it will take you some time to be attired correctly. I daresay you have no dresses appropriate for the position. I shall ask

Mrs. Hudson to acquaint you with the finer art of sewing clothing."

"What would you know about my wardrobe, or my sewing abilities, for that matter?" I was trembling with anger. "I shan't be in service to you or anyone else. I shall return to Corpus Christi if I must walk the entire distance." I left the study and returned to the bedchamber. My trunks not yet delivered, I found my carpet bag stuffed under the bed and began selectively packing, tears streaming down my face and wetting the front of my dress.

Elizabeth appeared at the open door, gaping at the scene before her. "Are you leaving us, Miss?"

"Yes, I am. Please ask Gump Hoss whether there is a horse available for my use. I shall not accept another hour of Mr. Pennyman's hospitality."

The maid did not reply but left me. I heard her footfalls in the hall and the rear stairway door opening and closing. I was locking the clasp on the bag when Mrs. Hudson swept into the room.

"Elizabeth tells me you are intent on leaving us. Has something transpired to put you in this frame of mind?" The housekeeper's countenance displayed concern.

I wondered at her sincerity. "Thank you, Mrs. Hudson, but I shall not burden you with my problems. I need the use of a horse. I shall see that it is returned to Gehenna upon my arrival at Corpus Christi." I looked at her while I spoke, hoping she would betray her true feelings.

Her face a mask, she looked out the open door and back into the room. "Wait here. I shall call for you." She hurried out the door, the echo of her receding footsteps reverberating in my ears. I looked about the dismal little room, turned, and began removing my belongings from the wardrobe and stacking them on the faded counterpane.

Elizabeth knocked softly on the open door before addressing me in a hushed tone, "Mrs. Hudson would like to speak with you in her sitting room."

"Please convey my regrets. I shall be leaving this ranch." I kept my voice even, cold, hard. "Were you able to speak with Gump Hoss?"

"Miss Llewellyn, Mrs. Hudson was quite insistent you should speak with her downstairs. Please come with me."

"Has Mr. Pennyman left the house?"

"No, Miss. He's still in his study. Please, Miss, do go to Mrs. Hudson," the maid implored, her face contorted in fear and anxiety.

I saw no alternative. With Josiah ensconced in his study, I would be unable to walk out the front door. Catching up my bonnet, shawl, and carpet bag, I followed Elizabeth down the back stairs to the entrance of Mrs. Hudson's sitting room.

The housekeeper sat in the rocking chair, staring into the empty fireplace. She turned at my gentle rap on the door and bade me enter. I shut the door and sat opposite her in the comfortable wing chair.

Seeing me settled, she said, "Mr. Pennyman has spoken to me. I do not know what has transpired between the two of you. It is not my business. He did inform me that your betrothal is broken, and you are to enter his service." She stopped for breath.

"Mrs. Hudson, I cannot stay here. I must leave as soon as possible. I wish it to be today."

"I understand, my dear." She kept her hands neatly folded in her lap but leaned forward ever so slightly and lowered the already soft volume of her voice. "We shall have to engage in a bit of intrigue to secrete you away from here.

But it will take some time to arrange."

"Who are 'we'?" I asked, desperately wanting to believe what the housekeeper was offering.

"You and me. And a few others. Please, believe me when I tell you that you would leave this minute were it within my power to arrange it."

"I see." Having been duped by Josiah, I was wary of her demeanor and speech. For the time being, I saw no choice but to go along with the older woman. "What do you want me to do?"

An hour later, when I left Mrs. Hudson, I went to the third floor. I had been in the servants' quarters only once and never thought I would find myself occupying one of the chambers.

Elizabeth was closing the door to a room and looked up when she heard my footfalls.

"Just in time, Miss. This shall be yours." She opened the door for me to enter. "I have moved your possessions. I just finished putting them away."

"Well, not quite. There are more in my bag," I replied, setting the carpetbag on the table and unlocking it.

"Not to worry. We shall put all to rights in a jiffy." As I pulled items out of the bag, she efficiently put them in their places. We were done in less than five minutes.

"All right, then. Shall we get you into this work dress? We do want Mr. Pennyman to believe you in service."

So focused had I been on the carpet bag that I had failed to notice a corded petticoat and brown work dress laid out on the bed.

As I was changing clothes, my stomach made a horrendous noise. "Did you break your fast this morning,

Miss?" Elizabeth asked.

"No. I had a disagreeable conversation with Mr. Pennyman and returned to my room. I had no thought of food."

"You must eat. We shall go down and ask Mrs. O'Malley for something to get you through the remainder of the morning."

I was self-conscious sitting at the servant's common table but dutifully ate the light repast placed before me. Mrs. Hudson came in and sat across from me, her brow furrowed.

"I am pleased I don't have to teach you to sew," she teased. "Mr. Pennyman has suggested a number of tasks for you, all the most unpleasant and unsuitable for any indoor servant."

My curiosity was piqued, but I decided against asking what he thought appropriate for me to undertake.

"We must make him believe you are behaving as a maid. It is out of the question that a lady, such as yourself, should engage in such work. Do you have anything in mind, Miss?" Mrs. Hudson fingered the items on her chatelaine.

"I am afraid I have none of the practical training in housekeeping and cooking most girls receive. I suppose Mr. Pennyman is correct that I have led a privileged life. I was the mistress of my father's home, supervising the indoor staff. I enjoyed gardening and could not help but notice the gardens around this house have been sorely neglected. The front garden makes such a poor impression, especially since the fire." I spoke quietly but firmly. "From a distance, the plants look past their prime. Perhaps I can breathe life back into some of them."

"I believe gardening a most suitable task for you,

provided you confine the activity to the mornings," Mrs. Hudson said as we rose from the long table. "It is much too hot this time of year for a lady to be toiling away under the afternoon sun. I'll show you to the gardening shed."

We left the house through the back door, into the courtyard, and entered a small building. I gathered the tools I wanted in a basket I found on a shelf and a watering can and walked with Mrs. Hudson toward the front of the house, passing the kitchen garden.

Seed packets were skewered on small sticks at the ends of once neatly furrowed rows. Fledgling plants and weeds were wilted and dying in the scorched earth.

"Mr. Pennyman told Mrs. O'Malley she was to tend this garden, but she has no talent for growing anything. If we depend on her, there will be no fresh vegetables. Jenkins replanted it a few weeks ago and has been tending it in his spare time."

"Where is the well?" I inquired. "These plants need water if they are to survive."

Mrs. Hudson pointed off to our right. "The pump is over yonder."

Dropping the basket, I took the watering can and marched to the pump. Mrs. Hudson returned to her duties while I spent several hours tending the failing plants.

Sitting back on my heels, I surveyed the now neat rows, satisfied with what I saw. Despite wearing leather work gloves, I could feel the dirt under my fingernails. It had been many weeks since I had sunk my hands into the earth, and it felt good.

Concluding my work in the kitchen garden completed, for the time being, I walked to the front of the house and started on the garden around which the drive curved. Not all the plants had burned, though most were singed on the edges. I was bent to the task, breaking up the hardened soil that many days and months without water had created, when Mrs. Hudson came out the front door and down the steps.

"Good heavens, Miss," Mrs. Hudson exclaimed. "I thought you were still in the back. The kitchen garden has never looked so fine. Mrs. O'Malley will be pleased. The dooryard has been an eyesore for as long as I remember. Jenkins hasn't time to nurture this garden properly. I'm afraid those roses have bloomed their last."

"Thank you, Mrs. Hudson. It is nice to shake the cobwebs out of my bones. I think the kitchen garden has been saved." I stood and arched my back to work out the soreness. "Mrs. O'Malley's talents are in the kitchen. She shouldn't have to concern herself with growing the vegetables. Is there someone on the ranch I could talk with about replanting this garden?

"Such a discussion could be enlightening for me, but might also serve to show Josiah that I was acquiescing to his edicts."

"Jenkins, perhaps. I will get a message to him that you wish to speak with him." She continued to admire the small accomplishments in this garden. With a start, she pointed toward the driveway. "Land's sake, it looks like we have a visitor."

Following her finger, I saw a small buggy pulled by a single horse ambling up the driveway. The unexpected guest had not yet reached the turn to come to the front of the house.

"I must be a sight after crawling through gardens all morning," I mused, looking at my apron and hands while gathering the tools. "I'll leave you to greet Mr. Pennyman's visitor."

"Uh, yes, of course," Mrs. Hudson slowly responded. She looked flustered with this unexpected occurrence.

I walked rapidly around to the back of the house and put away the gardening tools. After brushing at the dirt clinging to my dress and apron, I quickly washed my face and hands at the pump. With a cursory wipe of my boots on the scraper outside the back door, I let myself in through the service entrance and seated myself at the common room table.

Mrs. Hudson came downstairs, holding a silver salver, bearing a *carte de visite* with one corner carefully folded up. She extended the small platter, and I took up the card.

Mr. James Kilpatrick, Esq. was embossed on the crème colored card.

I had been acquainted with a man by that name in Connecticut. He was a few years my senior. We had attended the same church, and I had seen him at social events and even danced with him. "Who is he here to see?" I enquired.

"He asked for you by name," Mrs. Hudson responded with curiosity written on her face. "He is in the sitting room."

"Did he say anything else?"

"No, Miss."

"Thank you, Mrs. Hudson. I will see him. But, I want to make myself presentable." I ran up the three flights of stairs and into my room. I pulled clothing from the wardrobe and hurriedly changed into the first day dress that came to hand. I did not stop to change shoes. The work boots would be unseen under the dress. A glance in the mirror gave no hint of any dirt smudges on my face. With a hasty swipe of the hairbrush, a brooch quickly affixed at my throat, and I prayed I was well enough turned out to receive company.

I returned to the common room to find the housekeeper standing by the table. I walked past her, stopped, and turned toward her. "Mrs. Hudson, I think it best that Mr. Pennyman know nothing about Mr. Kilpatrick's visit." She nodded agreement as I turned and walked toward the staircase to the first floor.

Tall and lean, James Kilpatrick stood in front of the fireplace with his back to the door when I entered. "Mr. Kilpatrick?" I asked.

He turned around and strode across the room, "Miss Priscilla Llewellyn. How wonderful to see you again." He grasped my hands and smiled after making a shallow bow.

I looked into his face at the familiar angular features and startling emerald green eyes. "I heard that you did not return to Connecticut after the war. How did you come to be in Texas?"

He looked kindly at me. "During the Battle at Antietam, I became separated from the Fourteenth Connecticut. I attached myself to a company from New York. We wandered around, chasing the Rebs through the Southern states for more than a year. Somewhere in all that fighting, I was reassigned to a company from Iowa. We marched west from Mississippi in '64 and were attacked by Confederates in Arkansas. I never did learn what outfit they were in. The Rebs overran us, and I was captured. They forced marched us to their outpost. When word of General Lee's surrender came, they released us.

"I found myself partial to the Texas climate and decided to stay. After traveling around the state a bit, I settled in Corpus Christi and opened a law office." He opened a case he had placed on a chair. "I have a letter of introduction from your father." Mr. Kilpatrick extended his right hand, holding out a large envelope. "He was uncertain whether you would remember me. Mr. Llewellyn asked that I provide you with certain documents."

"I wonder how Papa learned you were here." I mused, taking the envelope from him.

"My family, most likely. Our fathers were partners in a lumber mill for many years. Mr. Llewellyn wrote to me some months ago, explaining the situation and requesting my services. I am delighted to be of service to both of you."

I started to open the envelope, stopped, thought a moment, and asked. "Mr. Kilpatrick, what do you know of Josiah Pennyman?"

"Not very much, I must confess. I understand he is quite wealthy. He's been in Corpus Christi long enough to build up this ranch. He has not endeared himself to the hostesses of the community by declining every invitation extended to him. Gossip and rumors run rampant.

"Certainly, as his betrothed, you know more about him than I?" The question showed on his face.

"Papa arranged the marriage. Josiah and I had not met until I arrived here two weeks ago," I confessed. "I expected to be wed as soon as I came into the city, but Josiah sent Percival Templeton to meet the ship. Everything seemed to go well initially but now it seems to have gone terribly wrong. There will be no marriage. There is much I wish to relate to you, but there is no time. At the risk of sounding like a character in a melodrama, it is not prudent to discuss these matters within these walls.

"I prefer you take this back without my inspection." I held out the unopened envelope. "I have told Josiah I know nothing of Papa's business affairs, which is true. It is best that I remain ignorant until I am safely away from Gehenna."

Alarm replaced the smile on his face as he took the envelope from me, returning it to his case. "Are you in danger, Miss Llewellyn?"

"I do not believe so, as long as I do as I am told." My mind was racing. *Should I ask Mr. Kilpatrick to take me to Corpus Christi?* I struggled to stay calm and keep my voice even. I hoped he didn't notice my hands trembling.

"You ought to leave. Now. It would not bode well for Josiah to find you here. He has a violent temper. I cannot imagine his reaction should he find us together."

He lifted the case from the chair and started toward the door. "As you wish." Concern showed on his face and in his voice.

I walked with him from the parlor toward the front door.

Mr. Kilpatrick looked at me, concern writ large on his face. "Would you like to return to Corpus Christi with me? It would not be an inconvenience."

Standing in the center of the foyer, I looked at the attorney. "I wish nothing more at this moment, but no. Josiah would surely track me down in the manner of hunting runaway slaves. I have no desire to bring trouble to your doorstep." I looked down at my hands, hoping he didn't notice the dirt under my fingernails. "He says my father wronged him in some business dealing during the rebellion and that Papa owes him money. He reasoned that he would gain control of Papa's holdings by marrying me.

"Josiah now knows that Papa sold everything and sailed to Africa. He believes Papa took his wealth with him and that I have nowhere to go. I think it to my advantage that Josiah believes me to be penniless." We stopped at the front door.

"Josiah Pennyman is a powerful and vindictive man. I might go so far as to describe him as evil. He would surely have no qualms of harming anyone coming between himself and his desires." I opened the door, and we stepped onto the porch. The day was warming, felt even in the shade. "He is leaving Saturday next and will be away for two months. Would I be imposing on your kindness to ask that you return for me in a fortnight?"

"If you are certain," Mr. Kilpatrick said, doubt in his voice. "I must admit I am not convinced you should remain under this roof."

"I am certain that I cannot have Josiah Pennyman's wrath visited upon you. Nor do I want him to know the contents of that envelope." I longed to confide in this man from my past, but I knew it would be dangerous for him to linger at Gehenna. "You must leave. *Now*. I shall look for you in a fortnight."

"I shall be here, Miss Llewellyn. You may depend upon it."

I watched him descend the steps, remove the strap that hobbled his horse, and climb into his buggy, but went inside and shut the door before he drove away. I fought the urge to seek refuge with him. Instead, I returned to the third floor.

I sat on the bed and prayed that Mrs. Hudson was the only person to have seen James Kilpatrick. I feared whatever retribution should befall Mrs. Hudson and me should Josiah learn I received a gentleman caller.

Unnerved by his sudden appearance at Gehenna, questions flooded my mind. Almost without thought, I stood and began undressing. *How trustworthy is Mrs. Hudson? And what about the others? Are they loyal to Josiah?*

The day dress and crinoline lay in a heap on the floor around my feet. As I stepped out of them, I felt tears well up and threaten to escape. Staring at myself in the looking glass, I told the image there was no time for such a display.

There is much to consider and many plans to be made.

I appeared at dinner wearing the dirty work dress and apron. Rather than take my usual afternoon rest, I disregarded Mrs. Hudson's admonishment and returned to the dooryard, weeding and watering in a vain effort to salvage the plants not consumed in the fire.

As I stabbed at the dry soil, forcing it to release its hold, I felt the tears return. Alone under the Texas sun, my face hidden by the broad brim of my hat, I let them fall. *How did I come to this? How would I escape this horrible place? What would Papa say, seeing his daughter reduced to the status of a servant?* It was all too much. Surrendering to fear and confusion, I buried my face in the filthy apron and wept.

When I trusted my lower limbs to bear my weight, I gained the steps to the house and sat in the shade of the wide porch, composing myself before facing the women with whom I now resided.

Concern that news of my visitor would reach Josiah's ears was soon pushed to the back of my mind as my days were filled with learning to change bed linen, dust furniture, and hang laundry. Mrs. Hudson was displeased that I embraced the role of apprentice housemaid, believing that I should want to continue to behave as an honored houseguest despite Josiah's demands. She grudgingly gave up the argument after Mrs. O'Malley chanted, "Idle hands are the Devil's workshop," every time she saw the housekeeper.

I could not spend every day in the gardens and welcomed the tasks. Not that I would have indulged in the dark angel's work, but it was easier to move through the days with something—anything—to keep my hands and mind busy. I was gaining a new appreciation for servants and the burdens placed on them by the families they served.

Most everyone on the ranch was involved in preparations for the cattle drive. I came into the common room Thursday morning to find the cook and a man I had never seen poring over a paper on the table.

Mrs. O'Malley looked up at the sound of my footfalls but returned her attention to the conversation with the stranger without acknowledging me. They spoke in soft tones while pointing at the writing on the page.

I sat at the opposite end of the table and began to mend a hole burned into a tablecloth.

Their conversation concluded, and Mrs. O'Malley took the paper with her as the two left the common room. I heard the outside door open and close and watched through the big window as the man crossed the courtyard toward the outbuildings. A few minutes later, he returned, pushing a flatbed cart, with Gump Hoss walking alongside. They came through the hall and directly into the kitchen.

There was a murmur of voices, a grunt, and a groan, and Gump Hoss retraced his steps to the courtyard, carrying a large sack of flour. The other man followed, carrying a bag of rice. They both made several trips to and from the kitchen, loading food stores onto the wagon. When they were done, Mrs. O'Malley bustled the two men into the common room, followed by Amparo, carrying a tray of coffee and rolls, still hot from the oven. They fell on the rolls as though they had not eaten in a fortnight, liberally spreading butter and honey over the steaming bread.

Gump Hoss looked over the rim of his cup, espying me for the first time since he had come into the house.

"Good morning to you, Miss Llewellyn," the grandfather said. "You'll not have met Jenkins, have ya?"

"Good morning, Gump Hoss. It is always nice to see you. We have not had the pleasure of being introduced, though I have heard his name," I replied brightly.

Gump Hoss performed the introductions with a bit more flourish than necessary, particularly under the circumstances.

"Will you be going on the cattle drive, Mr. Jenkins?" I enquired.

"Yes, Miss. I'm the cook." Jenkins responded. He seemed a genial man. "We jes loaded up the provisions. I seen what you done in the gardens. Theys lookin' right fine now. Them vegetables Mrs. O'Malley wants will be real nice in a few weeks.

"I hear tell ya'll want ta grow sumpun in that thar round patch in the dooryard."

"Mrs. Hudson promised she would send a message to you. Something must be done to improve its appearance."

"Such jawin' would be a pleasure, Miss, if'n I weren't goin' on this drive. I'm sorry there ain't no time, with all still needin' to be done twixt now 'n Saturday."

The room fell silent, the only sounds coming from the kitchen.

The men finished eating and stood to leave. "Good day to ya, Miss," Gump Hoss offered, nodding.

"Good day to you both," I replied.

Jenkins nodded but said nothing. They turned into the hall, passed through the door, and out into the courtyard. Gump Hoss walked beside the cart as Jenkins pushed it back toward the barnyard.

Part 3
The Escape

Chapter 14

June 1866
Gehenna
Northwest of Corpus Christi, Texas

The cattle drive started before first light Saturday morning. A sense of anticipation drove me from my bed earlier than usual, though there was nothing for me to do for those leaving. Mrs. O'Malley and Amparo were bustling between the kitchen and the back door, plying the drovers with coffee and biscuits filled with meat and cheese.

I found Mrs. Hudson and Elizabeth sitting in the common room and joined them. We three watched shadowy figures rush about the courtyard, checking cinch straps and harness, ensuring the security of bedrolls, and shifting supplies in the wagon. I caught glimpses of the Master of Gehenna and heard his voice, though the words were indistinct.

Finally, above the din, we heard Josiah order the men to mount their horses and head out. Jenkins called to his mules, and his wagon creaked and moaned its way out of the yard, leading the train. Horses were released from their corral and carefully herded by the wranglers. They paraded toward the corral where the five hundred head of cattle had been kept this past week.

Josiah stopped his horse in front of the large window and purposefully looked in. Our eyes met, though I desperately wanted to avert mine. His face took on an evil appearance, with a ghoulish grin as he shouted through the glass, "You stay put. I'll deal with you upon my return." He spurred his horse and vanished into the darkness.

As they approached the prairies, an eerie silence descended over the courtyard. Looking at each other, the three of us released a collective sigh.

Odors wafting in from the kitchen proved our morning meal was being prepared. Elizabeth and I set the table in anticipation of breaking our fast.

Mrs. Hudson left and returned with a pot of tea. The three of us sat, sipping the aromatic brew and looking round the room. It was odd to know that we five were the sole occupants of the house. There would be no one for the indoor servants to care for during the next two months.

Our private thoughts were disturbed by Mrs. O'Malley and Amparo setting out breakfast. The decadence of a leisurely meal was not lost on the women with whom I shared the table. As we lingered over a last cup of tea, Mrs. Hudson said, "On to the next step of the plan."

Shaken, I looked at the housekeeper, unaware of who, other than Elizabeth and myself, had been included in her subterfuge.

I took a sip of tea, put down the cup, folded my hands in my lap, and returned my gaze to Mrs. Hudson. "I do hope your plans for me do not conflict with mine."

"I suppose that depends upon what you are determined to do," the older woman replied.

Uncertain whether to confide in these women, I kept silent. Mrs. Hudson, Mrs. O'Malley, and Elizabeth turned their attention to me. Amparo stared at her lap. I wondered how much of the conversation she understood or whether she simply chose to keep apart from it. I estimated her to be five or six years junior to me. As the quiet in the room grew, I decided it best to admit the appointment I had made earlier in the week.

"I am expecting a caller a week from Monday next."

Mrs. Hudson's countenance changed slightly. Elizabeth and Mrs. O'Malley looked at one another and back to me, curiosity writ large on their faces. Amparo displayed no sign of understanding. No one spoke.

The housekeeper pushed away from the table and stood, breaking the increasingly uncomfortable silence. "We all have things to do," she announced and turned, walking the few steps to the butler's office.

Elizabeth and Mrs. O'Malley moved in opposite directions while Amparo began gathering the dinnerware and serving pieces to be removed to the scullery. I followed Mrs. Hudson and stood in the doorway, waiting for the housekeeper to acknowledge my presence. She looked up from the drawer through which she had been rummaging.

"Yes, Miss Llewellyn? May I be of assistance?"

"I wanted to thank you for not speaking of my caller."

"There is no reason for the others to know that Mr. Kilpatrick has visited previously."

"He will be taking me to Corpus Christi."

"Will you return to your home?"

"No. There is no one and nothing left for me in Connecticut. I have not settled on a destination. I know only that I must leave this ranch and this state." My mind drifted to Ethan Brandt. *But I do not know where he is buried.*

Mrs. Hudson brought me back from my thoughts. "Now that Mr. Pennyman has left, I should think we may dispense with the charade of you laboring as a servant. It isn't fitting for a lady to be used in so sore a manner."

"I appreciate that, Mrs. Hudson. There is little else with which to occupy myself. I should prefer to continue with those small labors."

The housekeeper frowned in disapproval. "There is little for Elizabeth to do with Mr. Pennyman away. We will be closing up the house. We'll air it out and clean before he returns. In the meantime, we'll keep ourselves to the servants' quarters."

"Of course. I had thought only to continue as I have been to keep myself busy."

"Well, perhaps you could continue tending the gardens. Heaven knows what will become of them after you're gone."

Sensing the interview concluded, I thanked Mrs. Hudson, turned, and went to retrieve my hat and gardening gloves.

I stood, stretching my back and surveying the nice, neat rows of recovering plants in the kitchen garden. The scent of recently turned soil clung to my clothes.

"Looks like there'll be greens on the table soon." I was startled by the masculine voice behind me.

"Gump Hoss, what a lovely surprise to see you. The garden is coming along quite well. What brings you up to the house?"

"I come ta talk ta Mrs. O'Malley. The drive pert near cleaned out her pantry. I'll be goin' into Corpus Christi ta pick up supplies."

"Oh, when will you be going?" I tried to keep the tone casual while my mind raced.

"Not till next week. I got some work ta do afore I leave. I want ta make sure her stores don't go too short afore I kin git away."

"I see." I paused and regarded the grandfather before asking the favor I had in mind.

"I heared you and Mr. Pennyman had a fallin' out," he said in a gentle voice.

"Josiah has made his intentions clear. I am leaving Gehenna. I cannot stay under his roof longer than necessary."

"When ya leavin'?"

I had always felt comfortable with this kind man and had no qualms telling him what I had told the women over breakfast. He gave voice to concerns regarding Mr. Kilpatrick's honor, which I allayed by telling him about my caller. "Could you find your way to perform a small service for me?" I asked.

"Whatcha got in mind?" he replied, his eyebrows rising toward his hairline.

"Would you take my trunks to Corpus Christi?"

"Cain't think of a solitary reason not ta bring 'em along for ya. Where do ya want me to deliver 'em?"

"Mr. Kilpatrick will know where I am staying. You may call at his office when you arrive."

"Good 'nuff."

We walked to the house together. He turned into the kitchen while I went in search of Mrs. Hudson.

The trunks stood as silent sentinels in my room. Both were packed, ready for retrieval and loading into the wagon. A carpetbag sat on top of one trunk, awaiting the day it would receive those articles I would require while traveling to the seaside city.

As Mrs. Hudson had predicted, following a frenzy of activity early in the week, the house staff was enjoying more leisure time.

By Friday, Elizabeth and I had gone through the house,

room by room, covering furniture, closing, locking and shuttering windows, and drawing the draperies.

Mrs. Hudson, Elizabeth, Mrs. O'Malley, and I sat in the common room. We were all engaged in needlework. A pitcher of lemonade and a plate of cookies sat on the table. Elizabeth stopped to refill her tumbler. She gasped, nearly upsetting the pitcher as she stared out the window. The three of us followed her gaze, all stunned at the tableau before us.

Amparo was sitting in the gazebo with Mr. Templeton seated on her left, their bent heads nearly touching. Her hands were neatly folded in her lap. As we watched, his right hand covered both of hers. I looked away just long enough to glimpse the astonished expressions on the faces of my companions and returned my gaze toward the window. The couple seemed quite intimate.

"Well, I'll be," Mrs. Hudson murmured. "Who would have thought?"

"Never in my wildest imaginings," whispered Elizabeth.

"So, the child and the cad are together. I wonder how long this has been going on," Mrs. O'Malley uttered in a hushed tone, causing us to look at her.

"What do you suppose they're talking about?" Elizabeth asked.

"Nothing good, to be sure," the cook replied. "If I'd known she'd taken up with that fiend, she would have been gone long ago."

"Now, Mrs. O'Malley," Mrs. Hudson interjected. "We must give the girl the benefit of the doubt. Mayhap she doesn't understand the nature of the man."

"She'd have to be thicker than pea soup not to know," Elizabeth observed. "He's as evil as they come."

Though the day was quite warm, I shivered and kept my own counsel.

“Well, there’s nothing for it, Mrs. O’Malley,” Mrs. Hudson said. “You’ll have to speak to the girl about the company she keeps. Word will get around like wildfire, and her reputation ruined before she can blink.”

“I’ve a feeling her reputation has already tumbled into the deep, Mrs. Hudson. I’ll call her in. It’s time to start supper.” Mrs. O’Malley rose from her chair. I heard her footfalls in the hall and saw her step into the courtyard and call to the kitchen maid.

The girl did not immediately acknowledge Mrs. O’Malley but remained in the intimate posture with Percival Templeton. They did finally stand, hands clasped together. He bent to speak into her ear. They embraced, he kissed her forehead, and she left the gazebo, glancing over her shoulder toward the man as she made her way to the house.

Mrs. O’Malley followed her through the hallway, neither speaking until they entered the kitchen. The familiar sounds of meal preparation prevented us from overhearing their conversation.

Mrs. Hudson, Elizabeth, and I picked up the assorted notions related to our sewing projects and set the table for the evening meal.

We did not speak again of the tryst until Saturday evening. Amparo was washing up after supper in the scullery when Mrs. Hudson invited Mrs. O’Malley, Elizabeth, and me into her sitting room.

It was with trepidation that we entered the housekeeper’s parlor, so grave was the set of her face. Mrs. Hudson stood at the door, her hand on the knob. As we settled ourselves, she shut and locked the door, further discomposing us.

Mrs. Hudson went to stand in front of the empty fireplace, facing us. Her hands were neatly folded at her waist. She looked at each of us in turn. "Ladies, there is no reason to look so fearful. No calamity has befallen us as yet." Her voice was calm and steady. "I have pondered the assignation we observed yesterday afternoon and see no good coming of it."

"I talked to the child," Mrs. O'Malley interjected. "I tried to tell her Templeton was no good and to stay away from him. She wouldn't hear a bad word about him. Said he'd been nice to her and her family. She won't say what they talked about, how long he's been back, or where he's staying. She denies there is anything between them, but she's known to tell fairie stories."

"What's he done for her family?" Mrs. Hudson asked.

"She refused to say," Mrs. O'Malley said.

"He frightens me," Elizabeth whispered. "I shall not feel safe in my bed, thinking he's wandering around the house."

"He's not tried to enter the house," Mrs. Hudson said.

"No, not yet," Mrs. O'Malley countered. "Do you know whether he still has a key?"

"Mr. Pennyman relieved him of it when he was dismissed." Mrs. Hudson reasoned.

"Lack of a key would not bar Percival Templeton's entry, should he have a mind to come inside," I said. "How well does Amparo understand English?"

"Well enough to understand my instructions," Mrs. O'Malley answered, considering the question. "I always liked that she wasn't a chatterbox. She does her job and keeps to herself."

"She never looks at anyone during meals. I always thought she had difficulty following the conversation. Now, I wonder..." Mrs. Hudson was looking at the door, allowing each of us to finish the sentiment.

"What's to be done, then? We've no man under this roof," Elizabeth said.

"Gump Hoss was up at the pump this mornin' when I was comin' back from the necessary. I told him what we seen," Mrs. O'Malley reported. "He said he'd put out the word to the field folk to keep watch for Mr. Templeton."

"Will that be sufficient to keep him from gaining entrance?" I asked.

"There's not much else to be done, what with Mr. Pennyman gone," Mrs. Hudson observed.

The room was silent, save the ticking of the mantle clock. As though by some unspoken consensus, we stood and followed Mrs. Hudson toward the door, which she unlocked and opened. We filed out to find other occupations for our hands and minds.

Chapter 15

Life inside the house continued. It was best to keep busy. I feared the tense atmosphere would fracture with disastrous results should the precise word be spoken or gesture made. We minded our tongues when Amparo was nearby, believing anything said within her hearing would be carried to Templeton.

Monday morning dawned bright and hot, without a breath of air. Still, I woke with a nervous excitement, anticipating the arrival of my rescuer.

There had been no communication with Mr. Kilpatrick since his visit, thus no method of knowing when he might arrive.

I had finally convinced Elizabeth I was capable of dressing myself and presented at breakfast wearing a clean work dress and apron and more carefully *coiffed* than had become my habit the past fortnight.

Excitement danced in Elizabeth's eyes as she took her place beside me. She reached over and squeezed my hand under the table, whispering, "You're leaving today."

I glanced at her, smiling, but had no opportunity to reply as Amparo came in to set plates of eggs and sausages on the table. She wore a blank expression and did not speak to either of us. A sense of foreboding swept over me, and I shuddered as a chill ran down my spine while the young maid returned to the kitchen.

“Are you well, Miss?” Elizabeth asked.

“Yes, quite. Someone just walked across my grave,” I replied.

Amparo returned, carrying more dishes, with Mrs. O’Malley following her and bearing a pot of tea. Mrs. Hudson bustled in from somewhere near the back stairs, fairly falling into her chair.

The meal was consumed with undue haste. No one lingered over a last cup of tea. Elizabeth and I helped Amparo stack the dishes, then went to the courtyard to begin the laundry. With the two of us working, we had the laundry washed, rinsed, and hung to dry before ten. The temperature increased as the sun arced across the sky, evaporating the moisture almost faster than it took us to pin the laundry to the line.

Elizabeth and I were ironing when we heard a bell ring. Looking up from our work, we noted it was the front doorbell. We both smiled.

“You go ahead, Miss. I’ll finish up,” Elizabeth said.

I carefully placed the flat iron on the stove and hurried from the room. I waited for Mrs. Hudson in the common room. I had begun to doubt James Kilpatrick had arrived when the housekeeper came downstairs and extended the small tray upon which lay a *carte de visite*.

“He’s in the sitting room,” she said as I took up the card. “I opened the room before breakfast. We couldn’t have you receiving a gentleman caller with dustcovers on the furniture, could we?” I looked from the lawyer's image on the CV to Mrs. Hudson and smiled. The older woman returned the gaze, her eyes sparkling.

“He is a very handsome man, Miss,” she said in a

conspiratorial tone and with the corners of her mouth turned up.

"Yes, I know," I responded, placing the card in my apron pocket and taking the stairs to the first floor.

When I opened the sitting room door, James stood at one of the windows, facing the ruined dooryard, his hands linked behind his back, under his frock coat. I studied his strong, handsome profile.

"Good morning, James. We did not expect you before dinner. Did you travel overnight?" I entered the room, quietly shutting the door behind me.

He turned toward me, extending both hands in greeting, "Good morning, Priscilla. No, I passed last night with friends and traveled the remaining miles this morning. We shall stay with them tonight and go on to Corpus Christi tomorrow."

"Please, sit," I said, taking a seat on a divan opposite two chairs beneath a window.

"Thank you, but I prefer to remain standing a while longer if you don't mind."

"I do understand. Long overland journeys can be taxing on a body."

As I contemplated my next comments, Mrs. Hudson entered with a tray of lemonade and sweet biscuits. "Dinner will be served at one, Miss," the housekeeper advised as she set the tray between James and me on a butler's table.

"Mr. Kilpatrick, would you mind dining downstairs? I shall explain." I watched Mrs. Hudson as the horror of my query played on her features.

The attorney replied, "As you wish, Miss Llewellyn."

"Mrs. Hudson, please ask Elizabeth to set a place for our guest. Thank you." My dismissal sent the woman bustling from the room.

When we were once again alone, James sat in one of the

chairs and asked, "What's happened here? Your attire and dining with the servants lead me to conclude you are in more difficulty than I feared."

I told him about the arranged marriage, the trip to Corpus Christi aboard the *Emma*, Percival Templeton's verbal abuses during the journey to Gehenna, and Josiah's ill-treatment of me after learning Papa had sold all of his holdings and sailed to Africa.

He sat with his long legs crossed, an elbow resting on the arm of the chair, chin securely in the palm of his hand. When I had finished, he accepted the lemonade I poured for him. He took a long drink and looked at the ceiling.

"That is quite a tale. I see now that you acted quite sensibly when we last met." Standing to look out the window, lemonade in hand, he continued with his back to me, "Are you acquainted with a Mr. Jacob Smythe?"

The question surprised me. "Why, yes. How is it you know of him?"

Elizabeth interrupted with the announcement of dinner being served. I led him downstairs and introduced him. Conversation during the meal was stilted, reminding me of my first meals with the servants.

"It's time you two were leaving," Mrs. Hudson observed as the mantle clock in her sitting room struck two.

"It is some distance to the Huber's farm, Miss Llewellyn," he said.

Standing up, I replied, "I shall be ready in a few minutes."

Elizabeth excused herself and followed me upstairs.

The women gathered around me as James secured my carpetbag under the seat of his buggy.

"Thank you, Mrs. Hudson," I said sincerely. "You came to my aide at one of my direst hours. I wish you the very best."

"It was my pleasure, Miss," the housekeeper responded. "I am sorry Mr. Pennyman treated you so sorely."

"Mrs. O'Malley," I began. "You are a marvelous cook. I shall be hard-pressed to find someone comparable wherever I settle."

"Thank you, Miss," her face reddened. "It's been a pleasure to know you."

I looked at the housemaid, tears welling. "Elizabeth, I believe I shall miss you most of all. You have become very dear to me. Do take care of yourself and the others."

"I shall, Miss," she responded, dropping a small curtsy.

I looked around, but Amparo was not in the dooryard. I wondered where she was and turned to look at James standing next to the buggy.

"Has anyone seen Amparo since I went upstairs?" I asked.

"Last I saw her, she was in the scullery," Mrs. O'Malley answered.

"Do you think she's still there?" *Is she with Mr. Templeton?*

"Miss, are you all right?" Elizabeth asked. "You're quite pale."

"Yes...yes," I stammered.

James Kilpatrick was at my side in an instant. "What is it, Miss Llewellyn?"

"A disturbing thought crossed my mind. Shall we depart?"

He assisted me into the buggy. The three women watched as the conveyance rounded the garden and turned into the drive toward the road. I twisted around for a final wave to the servants and settled myself for the long ride.

As we passed under the archway announcing the name of this dreadful ranch, I saw movement out of the corner of my eye, causing me to stiffen and audibly take in air.

"What is it?" he asked.

"I thought I saw something in the scrub," I replied. "It was probably just an animal," I wondered who I was trying to convince.

After turning onto the road to Corpus Christi, the horses transported us away from Gehenna at a canter.

"Why did you ask about Jacob Smythe?" I enquired.

James looked at me. "How do you know him?"

In something just louder than a whisper, I said, "I owe him my life."

"What?" His exclamation was so loud startled birds sprang from scrub along the side of the road. "When? How?"

Visions of the ship's corridor leapt to mind. Crenshaw's fetid odors filled my nose. I began to tremble, and tears welled. I covered my face with my gloved hands. Willing the sailor from my thoughts, I retrieved a handkerchief from my reticule, making an effort to regain my composure.

"I am sorry. It is not my habit to weep over every little mishap," I said, dabbing at my eyes with the small square of cotton. "You wanted to know about Jacob. He rescued me from one of the sailors who was intent on doing me harm. Jacob is the purser on the *Emma* and would sometimes escort me to the captain's dining room."

"You dined with the captain?"

"Almost every night," I answered with impatience in my voice. "You did not answer my question: Why did you ask me about Jacob Smythe?"

"He came to my office some weeks past. Probably the week you arrived."

"I daresay that would be true. I am aware that he had ship's business in Corpus Christi."

"It was a curious visit. He came in without an appointment, anxious to see me. I had some time, so I saw him. He dropped a small parcel on my desk and asked that I hold it until Miss Priscilla Llewellyn called for it.

"The man refused to divulge the contents and was quite insistent that he was careful to follow your instructions. He was quite agitated."

I smiled, playing out the scene James described and hearing Jacob's voice in my mind. "He is a dear man. But, how did he know to come to you?"

"He said that your father had given his captain my name. Just what did you ask the poor soul to do?" the lawyer asked.

"I was uncertain of my betrothed's character and loath to allow him to claim ownership of the furniture that has been in my mother's family for generations. While the ship was docked in New Orleans, I asked Jacob to put it in storage where Josiah Pennyman could not gain access to it. After we were under sail to Texas, I realized that I had no immediate need for the winter clothing and a few other things I kept with me on the ship, and I asked him to put them in storage in Corpus Christi. I thought to retrieve them after I was wed."

"Not many women would know to do such a thing," he said.

"I am well aware that married women have fewer rights than the Negros. I spent a goodly amount of time during the voyage pondering Josiah Pennyman's character."

"I have heard stories of him and Percival Templeton, but I always took them with a grain of salt." He paused to negotiate a particularly tight turn. "Templeton's been bragging all around town that he's in charge of Gehenna while Pennyman's away."

I feared for the women I had left at that ranch and sent up a quick prayer for their safety.

The only sounds to be heard were the horse's hoofs striking the dirt track and the creak of the harness and buggy.

"Thank you for taking me away from that place," I whispered.

"Don't thank me yet. We're still a long way from Corpus Christi. We must be ever vigilant. I don't believe you will be safe until you have left Texas. There's a foreboding in my bones. The last time I felt like this was just before the Rebs took me prisoner."

I did not know how to respond. Fear gripped me, and I began to tremble. I willed myself to be strong, refusing to be one of those women who swooned in the midst of adversity. *Is Mr. Templeton waiting for us?* "How much farther to your friend's home?"

"Not too far. The Huber farm is halfway between Gehenna and Corpus Christi. I'm sure we'll be all right."

We stopped once to water the horse at a small stream and to tend to human comfort before returning to the well-worn track.

The sun was dipping toward the western horizon, the time of day when colors are the most vibrant but dark is lurking. As we both gazed past the horse's head at the arid land, we saw a flash of red, and orange, and yellow. I held my breath, waiting to hear the report of the firearm, but it never came. A second flash occurred a few minutes later. Again, no report followed.

I stiffened and looked at James, fearful of what lay ahead.

He turned his head, looking at the landscape. "We best get off this road," he said, urging the horse through a gentle right turn into the desert.

"Are we near the Huber's farm?" I asked.

"Yes. I know another route that will keep us off the main road. I don't know what we just saw, but I don't reckon it was anyone hunting for their supper."

I made no reply but listened to the creaking of the buggy and the crunch of the iron tires on the desert floor as it bore us toward our destination. Lights became visible in the gathering darkness as we passed a stand of trees, and the growing shape of a building appeared in the offing. Within a very short time, he drew the horse and buggy to a stop in front of a sturdy house with a broad, wrap-around porch.

The glow of lamplight shone from the windows, giving a welcoming feeling to the house. A short, lean man with graying hair came round the corner of the house into the dooryard. He held the stump of a pipe in his mouth but removed it before speaking.

"You make goot time, James." The man spoke with a gentle but distinct German accent. "Ute vill be pleased you returned before dark. She's getting the supper together."

"Good evening, Otto. Have you had any problems this afternoon? We saw gunfire not far from here." James had climbed down from the buggy and walked around to assist me as he spoke.

"Nein. Probably somevone hunting da coyotes for bounty." James did not contradict him.

"Otto, may I present Miss Priscilla Llewellyn, late of Gehenna and Connecticut. Miss Llewellyn, your host for the evening, Herr Otto Huber."

"I am pleased to meet you, Herr Huber," I said.

The farmer clicked his heels, took my left hand, bowed

slightly over it, and looked me full in the face, "I am happy to know you. Meine frau hass been looking forward to meeting mit you. She don't get to talk mit utter vimen too much." Looking at James, he added, "Do you need help mit zoes bags, James?"

"I can manage, Otto. Thank you."

Herr Huber offered his arm and escorted me into a small, well-appointed hall with James following.

The odors of food filled the hallway, and I realized I was quite ready for a meal. A woman I took to be Ute Huber burst through a door at the far end of the hall, platters laden with food in both hands.

"Ach, Otto, you don't tell me our guests art here," she chided. "I put zeese on das table and come back, *schnell*." She disappeared through another door, returning almost as quickly, wiping her hands on her apron.

James introduced me to the tall, slim woman with tendrils of white hair stuck to her glistening face.

"You vill vant to vash before you eat, yah? I take you to your room." The lady snatched my hand and towed me through the foyer and down another hallway to a lovely bedchamber. "Ve eat ven you kommen oot, yah," she declared, leaving me to my ablutions.

Supper was bountiful and delicious, though I was unfamiliar with some of the dishes served. Frau Huber told me they were receipts her mother taught her when she was a girl in the old country.

The couple was friendly and obviously fond of James. I learned they lived alone, their son was killed at Vicksburg, and their daughter married and living in Ohio. Herr Huber held five hundred acres. He grew vegetables and hay on a portion of it and kept a small herd of cattle on the remainder.

It had been an exhausting day, and James wanted to resume our journey early in the morning. I bid the three friends good night and retired to my chamber.

A slight breeze from the open window stirred the lace curtains and breathed across my skin. Gooseflesh rose on my upper limbs. The night was punctuated with sounds from the barnyard and of the creatures inhabiting the desert beyond, lulling me into a dreamless sleep.

I had no timepiece at hand with which to measure the hours or minutes I had slept. A cracking like gunfire, shouting, and something akin to singing startled me from my slumber. The fracas was not outside my window, and while disturbing, was not frightening to me after I listened for a short time. It sounded as though some of the Hubers' farmhands had over-imbibed. Nonetheless, slumber eluded me, and I lay in the bed listening to the uproar until I heard doors opening and closing.

After hearing the third door, I rose, my feet easily finding the house slippers I had placed on the floor beside the bed. I opened the chamber door and cautiously peered up and down the dark hallway. Frau Huber came scuttling in my direction. She saw me and stopped. A serviceable muslin nightdress was revealed under her unfastened dressing gown.

"Fräulein, don't trouble yourself. Otto vill put a stop to dis foolishness. Go back to bed unt your sveet dreams." Without waiting to see my retreat, she hurried off.

I shut the door and sat on the edge of the bed, the noises outside changing again. I recognized three voices, though not the words being spoken, sending chills down my spine, and I shuddered despite the warmth of the late spring night.

Silence prevailed, only to be shattered with a renewal of shouting and an indefinable cacophony. Indecision caused me to stand and sit several times, torn between obeying Frau Huber's instructions and my desire to know what was transpiring. Unable to stay alone in that room any longer, I donned a wrapper and made my way into the dark kitchen to stand next to my hostess, both of us transfixed by the spectacle beyond the window glass.

A pile of hay had been thrown down from the barn's loft and set on fire, lending an eerie glow to the tableau. Men were engaged in fisticuffs. Others were holding bottles, clubs, or guns. Corrals and pens had been torn apart. Animals ran in all directions, adding to the chaos. Tools and farm implements flew through the air from the open barn doors to land on the hard-packed soil of the barnyard.

Herr Huber and James were arguing with the silhouetted figure of Percival Templeton. I feared the Butternut Man would harm these two men, though I witnessed no threatening gestures on his part.

Frau Huber turned from the window, stirred the banked fire in her stove, and set the coffee pot on it to boil. She gently took my arm and set me in a chair at the kitchen table. The older woman moved about her darkened kitchen with the familiarity of many years of use, taking down sugar, cups, and saucers.

I continued to listen to the destruction of the barnyard, fearful that these men would set fire to the house or one of the outbuildings. I held myself erect and still, my hands folded tightly in my lap. Fear had crept into my bones, keeping me sitting in the chair.

Quite suddenly, as though someone else possessed my person, I leapt to my feet and found myself outside, standing very close to Mr. Templeton. “What is this about? What have these people done to you? Stop this foolishness at once,” I heard myself shout, glaring into the former butler’s face.

“Well, the snippet comes out to defend her man,” Percival Templeton sneered, moving his arms as though to grab me.

James was a moment quicker, clutching my arms and pulling me backward toward himself.

“Give me the girl,” Mr. Templeton growled. “She belongs to Mr. Pennyman. Bought an’ paid fer. I mean to return her to Gehenna.”

“Slavery is dead. She belongs to no one but herself,” James retorted, trying to steer me back to the house. I resisted, intent on confronting the Butternut Man. “That contract has been dissolved. She is no longer betrothed to Mr. Pennyman. She has every right to leave and go where she wishes.”

“No woman is her own person. Women belong to men, always have, and always will. Her father gave her to Mr. Pennyman. I heared that tale she told them wimen at Gehenna. It’s a passel of lies. Mr. Pennyman wouldn’t have let her go. She’s worth a fortune to him.”

“I’m afraid you are misinformed. Her circumstances have been altered. She is a pauper. Mr. Pennyman no longer wishes to marry her. No bans were ever read. Therefore, there is no contract.”

“That’s not the way of it. Mr. Pennyman wants her, all right. The wench is goin’ back. Give her to me.” Mr. Templeton’s harsh speech was enough to know he meant to have his way. The set of his jaw and the look in his eye was fearsome.

“No.” James leaned closer to me, speaking softly into my ear, “Run for the house. You and Ute hide. She’ll know where to go. I'll find you." He released my arms and pushed me aside, out of the Southerner's reach.

I wasted no time in running back inside the house. Out of the corner of my eye, I saw James and Herr Huber set themselves upon Templeton, keeping him from reaching me.

I found Frau Huber busy pulling ingredients from the pantry shelves and putting them on the table next to a large mixing bowl.

"We must leave. James said you would know where to go." I clenched her wrist and started to drag her through the house.

"Vhat ist happened?"

"That man means to return me to Gehenna. He will stop at nothing to do so."

"Dis vay." The German lady took the lead out the front door into the desert night, my hand still firmly grasping her wrist. The sounds from the barnyard faded away, with only the nocturnal noises of the natural inhabitants to accompany the soft whisper of our house shoes slipping through the sand.

Frau Huber took long strides, forcing me to walk quickly, tripping over unseen obstacles as she pulled me through the desert.

"Ve must hurry, *schnell, Fräulein.* Zat terrible man cannot haf you." I marveled at her calm manner, as though hiding young women was a frequent occurrence. "Zis vay." She pulled me along behind her as her long steps quickened.

An enormous shadow loomed in front of us, stirring a feeling of foreboding. As we approached the shape, I was able to ascertain it was a copse of trees. My guide entered with the appearance of great confidence while I followed with trepidation.

The older lady's footfalls slowed as she entered the grouping, stopping all together near a ring of trees at the center of the stand. She looked about in a manner I had seen hunters do when taking their bearings and started off again with renewed determination. We came to a large rock, turned, and walked toward a tree that appeared no different than all the others but obviously had some significance to Ute Huber. She stooped, plucking something from the base of the tree, turned once more, and walked through the thicket to the other side, to a small wooden structure, no more than a shack.

The farmer's wife wrenched her limb from my hand and walked around the small building twice. Satisfying herself, she used the object she had picked up to unlatch the door. As she opened it, she pushed me inside and bolted the door. She guided me through the dark room to a chair. I sat, hearing some shifting about, the strike of a lucifer and the hissing of it igniting. The flame of a candle flared, then settled to stand sentinel.

The windowless building was one room, sparsely furnished with a table, two chairs, a double bed, and a small china cupboard. There was no fireplace or other visible means of cooking or heating.

"Where are we?" I asked.

"Ve are safe," Frau Huber answered as she opened cupboard doors and began rifling through the contents. "Ve stay here until Otto comes." She placed a tin of crackers on the table. Returning to the cupboard, she brought a wheel of cheese, a knife, plates, and cups. From a corner, she brought forth a jug of water.

"Ve eat. No goot hunger *haben.*"

We ate, each keeping to herself. Rather, she ate. I picked at the food, rearranging it on the plate from time to time. I watched this woman, marveling at her calm exterior, and wondered what caused her to leave her country to come to this inhospitable place.

"You rest, Liebling," Frau kindly led me to the bed and drew back the quilt. After tucking me in, she returned to the table and sat, watching the door.

As realization that we were safe settled on me, the tension drained away, and sleep slowly overtook me.

A curious combination of knocking and scratching brought me back from slumber. I sat up as Frau Huber responded with her own peculiar code. Receiving an appropriate response, she lifted the bolt and opened the door, admitting Herr Huber and James Kilpatrick.

Sunshine splashed across the floor through the open door but was quickly swept away as Herr Huber closed and secured it from intruders.

"You are well, Fraulein?" the German gentleman asked.

"I am unharmed," I replied, tightening the sash on my wrapper, self-conscious that I was wearing no underpinnings. "And you, Herr Huber, I trust you are uninjured?"

"Ya, I am goot. James, he has some scratches, just a little blood."

"I am relieved." I found myself looking toward Frau Huber, who stood near her husband, looking pensive.

"Vat vas zee soldier looking for in our barn? Vy vas he swrowing sings about?" the farmer's wife asked.

"It's a long story, Ute. But, the short of it is that Templeton claims Miss Llewellyn is responsible for his banishment from Gehenna and wants his revenge against her. He saw us drive into your place and thought to make a ruckus as subterfuge to entering the house. I don't know whether he means her harm, but he doesn't want to take her to a church social," James said, looking at each of us in turn.

Herr Huber took up his wife's hand and patted it. "I vill tell you zee whole story after zee young people leave."

"I am grieved to have brought this trouble on you. I should not have accepted your hospitality. I shall not tell stories out of school, but rest assured that Mr. Templeton's dismissal was justified," I whispered.

"Let us return to zee haus. I vill start zee meal," Frau Huber said and started to leave the little cabin.

"Is it safe for us to return?" I asked.

"Yes. Templeton and his people were persuaded to leave the farm," James assured us.

"Mine shotgun vas zee reason for his leaving," declared Herr Huber, wearing a satisfied expression, and patting the weapon cradled in the crook of his arm.

Chapter 16

The front of the house looked as it did when James and I arrived the previous day. Frau Huber walked straight through the house to look at the barnyard beyond. She stopped in the doorway, taking shallow breaths as though it was difficult to move the air into her lungs.

Coming up behind her, I stood to her left, gasping as I scanned the carnage. The scene could have been the subject of one of Matthew Brady's famous photographs.

"*Mine Gott in Himmel.* Zee yard looks like zee battlefields," the farmwife uttered.

I was heartbroken for this couple. They had worked hard to build this farm. I had no words with which to comfort the older woman. *This calamity never would have befallen these gentle people had I not come here.* Quietly, I went to the bedchamber, dressed, and prepared to resume our journey.

There was no lively conversation over the abundant morning meal. Our speech was subdued, as though speaking loudly would bring back the men who had wrought havoc in the barnyard.

Perhaps James is right about Mr. Templeton still being on Josiah's payroll. Would the Butternut Man have taken matters into his own hands were he not still employed at Gehenna*?*

When we had all eaten our fill and were leaving the dining room, I spoke to James. "I do believe we should be on our way as quickly as possible."

"Yes, I quite agree," he said. "We are already leaving later than I planned. We have quite a long drive ahead of us. I had hoped we would be in Corpus Christi in time for dinner. That time has passed. We may now arrive before supper."

I was dismayed when James' buggy was brought around to the front of the house. The bonnet covering was cut to ribbons and hung limply over the seat, which had also been damaged. Stuffing protruded from the cushions. Seeing the expression on my face, he said, "It could have been worse. Otto and I looked at the undercarriage and wheels. As far as we can tell, they were not damaged."

We said our final goodbyes to the Hubers and boarded the buggy. James guided the horse onto the road toward Corpus Christi.

The sun was making its way to the top of the sky. The day was warm, with dark, threatening clouds gathering on the horizon. I prayed we would reach the city before the storm broke.

We spoke little at first but then took turns relaying our experiences during the early morning melee. The discussion turned to what I should do once in Corpus Christi. It was clear that I would not be safe so long as I was within reach of Josiah Pennyman or his henchmen.

"You do need to deal with the legal matters we spoke about a fortnight ago," he said.

"Yes, I suppose I must." It was difficult for me to think of what my father had left behind, as though he was in the graveyard rather than halfway round the globe. I could not think of him in those terms. I wanted to remember him in better times when he was not stricken with the guilt of his actions or inactions during the war.

The conversation lapsed. I listened to the cadence of the

horse's hooves on the dirt path. There was a sudden screeching, metal on metal, accompanied by the buggy violently shaking and tilting, causing James to fall against my left side as the right wheel left the axle and fell to the ground.

We looked at each other, the horror and gravity of the situation gripping us both. He gingerly disembarked and assisted me in doing the same. Our gaze wandered from the buggy to its dismounted wheel for some moments. Both of us were mute, and our feet frozen to the places where we stood.

I finally gathered the courage to ask, "Can you repair it?"

"I don't know. I'm not certain what happened. Otto and I looked at the wheels this morning and found no damage." He walked back to the wheel, bent down, and began looking at it on the ground. He moved to the other side of the buggy to look at the wheel still attached to the axle. He walked back along the track, looking down as he went. He stopped, picked up something, inspected it, shook his head, and returned to where I stood.

He held out a small piece of wire, coiled like a spring. "It looks like the nut holding the wheel on the axle was removed. I think this piece of wire was put in its place. I'll need to work out how to secure the wheel to get us back to the Hubers."

"We cannot go back there. I have brought enough trouble to their doorstep." I wanted no part in bringing more hardship to those lovely people.

"Well, whether we go forward or backward is of no moment if we cannot get this wheel back on the buggy. We shall have to work out a way to hold up the buggy to reinstall the wheel," James sagely pointed out.

As we pondered this new problem, the sound of horses on the road came to our ears. We both looked in the direction of the noise. I was relieved to see Gump Hoss sitting on the seat of a wagon. Hoops had been installed and covered with canvas, making it look like the wagons people used to traverse to the west.

The grandfather guided his team off the road behind our disabled conveyance.

"What ails yer buggy, Mr. Kilpatrick?" Gump Hoss asked, stepping down from his perch.

"It appears the nut came off the wheel," Mr. Kilpatrick replied. "I could use your help setting the wheel back on the axle."

"How'd that happen?"

"I believe it had help."

"Anyone you know?"

"Yes, I am sure of it. But I'll not be naming names at present. I want to get back on the road."

"I have some odds and ends in the wagon that might be useful. Let's get that axle off the ground and cleaned up. I'll get my jack."

Gump Hoss returned to the wagon. I heard him put down the tailgate and the scraping of boxes along the floorboards. I heard him speaking and thought he was talking to himself.

As he came round his wagon, carrying the wagon jack, Gump Hoss said, "Miss Llewellyn, you might be interested in somethin' I'm carryin'. Jes go on back and take a look."

I obliged the kind man and walked toward the wagon. As I passed the side of the conveyance, I heard a sound familiar to me but out of place in this vast desert. I made my way around to the back, leaned over the tailgate, and peered into the relative darkness of the wagon. To my surprise, Mrs. Hudson, Mrs. O'Malley, and Elizabeth sat on trunks and boxes.

Mrs. Hudson smiled. "Good day to you, Miss Llewellyn."

“What are you all doing here?” I asked, incredulous but pleased to see them.

“We talked about you leaving and couldn’t think of a single good reason for any of us to stay on. I don’t know why I remained as long as I did,” Mrs. Hudson explained.

“When did you leave? Where are you going?” I persisted.

“Before first light this morning,” Mrs. Hudson explained. “We’ll go into Corpus Christi for now. Then, we don’t know. None of us has family hereabouts anymore. We’ll stay at Mrs. Dolan’s boardinghouse while we decide where to go.”

“Come on up in here, Miss, get out of the sun.” Elizabeth beckoned.

Taking a box from the back, I put it on the ground and climbed into the wagon. I found a seat on top of one of my trunks. A feeling of well-being overcame me as I looked at the women I never expected to see again. I suddenly realized how fond of them I had become in such a short period of time.

“What happened to Mr. Kilpatrick’s buggy?” Elizabeth asked.

The women listened, making small exclamations, as I told them of the events of the previous night, concluding with the wheel coming off the buggy.

“Mrs. Huber is a lovely woman,” Mrs. O’Malley observed. “I knew her afore I come to work for Mr. Pennyman. She’s a very good cook.”

“She was so generous to open her home to me,” I observed. “And I repaid that generosity by bringing terrible calamity to her backdoor. I should never have involved Mr. Kilpatrick or the Hubers in my problems.”

“Now, Miss, how was you to know Templeton would do such a thing?” Mrs. O’Malley reasoned.

“I should have known Josiah would have me watched

while he was away," I said. "Who else would he trust? I have not met anyone else on that ranch who would undertake such despicable deeds."

"Oh, there are several, I assure you, Miss," Mrs. Hudson stated. "They are mostly cowboys, but a few work the fields. You were fortunate never to have encountered them."

Gump Hoss came to the back of the wagon and peered in. "Mr. Kilpatrick's ready to move on, Miss."

"Thank you, Gump Hoss," I replied and moved to leave the wagon. As I stepped onto the desert floor, I looked back at the women, "I hope to see all of you in Corpus Christi before we go our separate ways."

"I'm sure you will," Mrs. Hudson replied.

As I gained the seat of the buggy, Mr. Kilpatrick smiled at me. "You look contented."

"I am. I learned that something good came of this ugly affair."

"Yes, Gump Hoss told me. I'm pleased they decided to leave."

After a brief pause, I asked, "Will the repair hold until we get to Corpus Christi?"

"I certainly hope so. He found some parts in his toolbox that will hold it in place for the time being. I'll take the buggy over to the wheelwright after I get you settled at Mrs. Dolan's boardinghouse."

I looked at him, surprised to hear that name. "Gump Hoss is taking the women to Mrs. Dolan's."

"I'm not surprised. She runs the most respectable establishment in the city."

The horse settled into a nice, even gait, steadily bringing us closer to our destination. We passed through the arid plain with the wagon following.

We stopped near a copse of trees to partake of the meal

Frau Huber had pressed on us. The place looked familiar, but I could not immediately think why.

As I went to find a private place, it occurred to me that this was where Gump Hoss, Mr. Templeton, and I had camped my first night in Texas. An uneasy feeling came over me as I recalled the Butternut Man's contempt.

I sat on a box, eating cold meat and cheese, watching the hobbled horses crop the small grass patches along the stream's edge. It was a perfect moment in which I could believe there would be no more trouble.

A bloodcurdling screech shattered the desert calm, causing everyone to stop what they were doing. The women, visibly shaken, moved closer together. James held a morsel of food partway to his mouth, dropped it on his plate, then stood and moved with some haste toward the buggy, muttering, "Damn Rebel yell."

Gump Hoss jumped up and dashed to his wagon and retrieved a rifle. He looked at James and asked, "Is that revolver all you got?"

"There's no room for anything larger in this buggy," the lawyer replied.

The teamster reached under the wagon seat and brought out another long gun, along with a hunting pouch. "Here, take this," he said as he handed them to James. "There's buck and ball in the pouch."

Looking around the area, Gump Hoss ordered, "You women get in the wagon. Push all those boxes and trunks around and hunker down in the middle as best you can."

We did as we were told. Mrs. Hudson, Mrs. O'Malley, and I climbed inside. Elizabeth put the box we used for a step into the wagon bed, then climbed inside, closing and latching the tailgate. We looked on, our mouths agape at her movements.

"I learned to do that on the trip from California to Texas," she said matter-of-factly.

Most of the cargo was already pushed against the sides of the wagon, but we stacked boxes against the front, behind the teamster's seat, and across the tailgate, making as much room as possible in the center for the four of us to crouch on the floor.

Time seemed to stand still, with no sign of anyone or anything stirring outside the wagon. Mrs. O'Malley and Mrs. Hudson huddled together, and Elizabeth held my hand while we waited. I strained to listen for any movement outside, but there was none to be heard. *Was this a matter of sound carrying long distances?* I had read of such a thing, though doubted the truth of it.

The sound of a rifle being discharged startled me out of myself. It was almost a relief to hear it, but there was no further gunfire. We heard James and Gump Hoss bring the horses to the conveyances. They spoke soothingly to the beasts as they hitched them.

"You women keep down. We're gonna try to run through these rowdies," Gump Hoss called to us as he climbed onto the driver's seat. With a snap of the reins and a command to the horses, the wagon rolled forward, rattling over the uneven ground as he guided them back onto the dirt track. We struggled to remain upright as he urged the team into a run.

Boxes and trunks shifted with every turn and bump in the road as the horses gained speed. A hat box bounced across a trunk and fell in Elizabeth's lap. She placed it on its edge between two boxes to keep it from being damaged.

The grandfather looked over his shoulder at us, "Keep

yer heads down. Don't want no stray rounds ta ketch ya."

With the wagon bouncing down the dirt track, we gave up on sitting and did our best to lie down. Having a mind of its own, my crinoline was a detriment to reclining. Without being able to see what she was doing, Elizabeth reached up between my over-petticoat and the crinoline. She found the waistband and unfastened the cage. I struggled to my feet, and the cage collapsed around my ankles. Mrs. Hudson pulled it toward herself and wedged it between two boxes and the side of the wagon to keep it out of the way.

We heard more gunfire, and Gump Hoss shouted coarse words as he applied the brakes, causing the horses to slow their pace and stop while the wagon slid sideways on the dry, hard track. The wagon rocked on its springs. A head appeared over the top of the tailgate and disappeared again.

"Over here, Mr. Templeton. They's wemin in this here wagon." The voice was unfamiliar to me.

Mrs. Hudson sat up. "Billy Timmers, what would your mother say if she saw you trying to steal away women?"

The young man looked over the tailgate and into the face of Mrs. Hudson's fearsome expression. "Beggin' your pardon, ma'am, my mama ain't got no say in who I associate with. 'Tain't none o' her affair."

"I doubt she would agree," Mrs. Hudson observed. "What have any of us done to be accosted on a public road in this manner?"

"Mr. Templeton says thar's a runaway needs returnin' to Gehenna. I'm jes' tryin' to hep him ketch 'er," the young man said defensively.

"No one ran away, and most certainly, none of us is owned by anyone at Gehenna." Mrs. Hudson had maneuvered herself through the tangle of bodies and skirts toward the back of the wagon and now had her face just inches from Billy Timmers'.

"Ma'am, I's jes doin' as I been told. I ain't never laid eyes on 'er till I looked in this here waggin. Mr. Templeton say she belong to Mr. Pennyman, bought and paid fer."

I was outraged to be spoken of in such coarse terms. *What did they mean? That I had been purchased by Mr. Pennyman?*

My thoughts were brought up short by hoofbeats and loud voices. I could hear Templeton shouting but heard nothing from James or Gump Hoss. *Had they been injured or captured?*

"Miss Llewellyn, thar ain't no cause fer ya to hide in that wagon. Come on out afore my boys have to hurt yer fancy man and the ol' feller." Mr. Templeton's voice carried clearly into the wagon.

I started to rise, not wanting harm to come to my companions, but Mrs. O'Malley pulled me down and held onto my arm to keep me from leaving the wagon and whispered in my ear, "You stay where you are, Miss. Gump Hoss knows what he's about."

Before I could respond, the wagon began swaying from side to side. Mrs. Hudson lost her balance and fell onto Elizabeth, who did what she could to assist the older woman in righting herself.

The crack of a rifle sounded, and the wagon was still for a few moments but began rocking again. I could see hands at the tailgate and heard mumbled voices. Scuffling sounds followed. Mrs. O'Malley's grasp on my arm slackened as I rose to look out over the teamster's seat.

Neither James nor Gump Hoss was in sight. A group of men surrounded Templeton. I could see his mouth moving but could not hear what he said. As I watched, the group broke up, coming toward the wagon. The tailgate was let down, and a pair of hands took out boxes, dropping them on the ground. The hands reached inside, caught a handful of skirt, and dragged Mrs. Hudson out. She lost her balance and fell in a heap on the dirt.

The housekeeper sputtered as she attempted to rise but was prevented from doing so by two men who pushed her back to the ground.

"That ain't her," Mr. Templeton said, contempt dripping from his voice.

"She's the first one we could get aholt of," a high-pitched voice whined.

"Jim, hogtie, that old woman. We'll take her with us, too."

The Butternut Man was near the back of the wagon but did not look in.

As Mrs. O'Malley, Elizabeth, and I moved closer together, sitting sideways near the front of the wagon, I thought about James and Gump Hoss but had no time to dwell on them. We huddled behind the boxes as far from the tailgate as possible. A hand touched my shoulder, and I jerked away, stifling a shriek. As I turned my head, I saw Gump Hoss, his right index finger in front of his lips, indicating we should remain quiet, while his left hand gestured for us to put our heads down. We quickly lowered our heads as the grandfather leveled his gun, aiming toward the back of the wagon. Even with my head below the tops of the boxes, I was able to see out beyond the open end of the wagon.

A man peered at us, reaching his arms inside, appearing ready to grasp whatever he could. There was a thunderous noise as flame leapt from the barrel of the gun. Smoke hung in the air, stinging our eyes and throats and coating our mouths with an acrid taste. I watched as the man staggered backward, holding his chest and screaming. He fell to the ground with blood streaming from his chest, nose, and mouth.

The bark of pistols and rifles, and shotguns surrounded us. From his position on the teamster seat, Gump Hoss directed Elizabeth to one of the boxes on her right. Following his instructions, she opened the box to find a short-barreled rifle with rolled cartridges and caps.

"Do you know how to use that?" the grandfather asked.

"My father taught me to use a rifle when I was ten," Elizabeth snapped as she deftly loaded the weapon and shoved a few cartridges into her dress pocket.

"Good. Keep them ruffians outta the wagon," he instructed and slipped off the seat, disappearing from my sight.

We heard the cracking of wood as Minié balls found the sides of the wagon. The canvas cover shuddered with percussions from the long guns. Shouting, fisticuffs, and gunfire conspired to deafen everyone in the midst of this mêlée.

Elizabeth took up a post on a box behind the driver's seat, facing the opened back, the butt of the rifle resting against her shoulder, with the barrel pointed downward. Mrs. O'Malley and I crouched at her feet and pressed our cheeks to the floorboards. As I raised up to reposition myself, a Minié ball tore through the canvas on one side and hit one of the staves, severing it. The canvas sagged and blocked our view of the fallen man, save his feet.

Another of Templeton's men came to the wagon, a wicked grin pasted on his face. He looked up as he prepared to gain entry. At the same time, the maid raised the barrel of her weapon and took aim at his chest. He quickly backed away. We heard Mr. Templeton admonish the young man for his cowardice, cursing and slapping and punching him. In time, the beating stopped, and the Butternut Man himself appeared at the tail of the wagon. Elizabeth again leveled the gun.

"Mr. Pennyman's goin' ta be mighty disturbed ta find ya missin' when he gits back, Miss Llewellyn," the former butler chided.

"He shall have to live with the disappointment. He made his feelings toward me quite clear prior to his departure," I replied.

"You belong to him."

"I belong to myself."

"Git outta this waggin. Now." Templeton brought up his right lower limb as he started to climb onto the tailgate. There was a bone-rattling crack as the wagon filled with smoke and the overpowering odor of brimstone. Elizabeth fell backward, striking her head on the driver's seat and losing her grip on the rifle. When the smoke cleared to a haze, we saw the Butternut Man stagger backward and fall, his legs lying across those of his comrade. Both men were silent.

The thuds and grunts of fisticuffs surrounded the wagon. There was occasional gunfire. Elizabeth pulled herself upright, stood, fought her way through the sagging canvas to the back, and peered cautiously around the canvas.

"I can hear Mrs. Hudson's voice. I think she's in the trees over near the creek. I'm going to bring her back here," Elizabeth declared as she began to clamber down.

"Elizabeth," I said, surprised at the calmness in my voice.

"Miss, I must," she answered, determination writ on her face.

"Take the rifle," I instructed as I picked up the weapon and handed it to her.

"Oh. Yes. Of course." The maid took up the gun, extracted a cartridge from her pocket, reloaded, and disappeared from our sight.

"Do you think Mr. Templeton is dead?" I asked Mrs. O'Malley.

"Don't worry yerself about that, Miss," she replied.

"I shan't grieve for him."

"Very few will. That 'un was as evil as they come," the older woman observed.

The fighting stopped as suddenly as it had started. The prevailing silence was nearly as deafening as the skirmish had been and more frightening. We had no idea what had transpired outside. Approaching footsteps brought us alert to our dilemma. Gump Hoss and James announced themselves before coming to the open tailgate.

"Anything amiss in here?" Gump Hoss asked, peering into the relative darkness.

"The Timmers boy took Mrs. Hudson," Mrs. O'Malley reported. "Elizabeth went to find her. Miss Llewellyn and I are not injured."

"Who killed Templeton?" James asked.

"Elizabeth," Mrs. O'Malley and I said in unison.

"Are you both unharmed?" I asked.

"A few bruises, s'all," replied Gump Hoss.

"I'm going to know I was in a fight tomorrow." James managed a weak smile. He was covered in dust, and the left sleeve of his coat had been torn off. "I haven't been in a fight like this since the war." He looked over his shoulder and moved away from the wagon, returning with Mrs. Hudson and Elizabeth.

I made my way to the tailgate to disembark.

"Stay where you are, Miss Llewellyn. You're safer in there," James stated. "Gump Hoss and I must straighten out the harness, check the horses, and inspect the wagon. Then, we have to find my horse and buggy. Banjo ran off sometime during all this ruckus."

Gump Hoss assisted Mrs. Hudson and Elizabeth into the wagon before tending to the horses.

The four of us huddled together and uttered reassuring platitudes.

Gump Hoss told us one of the draft horses had been wounded. He cleaned and applied an ointment to the injured rump, assuring us that it was just a crease and would likely leave a scar, but presented no impairment to the animal.

James rode with Gump Hoss on the driver's seat with a loaded shotgun across his knees and kept a watchful eye for ruffians, as well as his horse and the buggy.

We spoke very little during the journey into the city but clung to each other, silently praying there would be no further encounters with the Butternut Man's minions.

We arrived in Corpus Christi before sundown, many hours later than planned, but with no further interference. I could not stop seeing Percival Templeton staggering backward after being killed. I had never seen a person shot and wondered whether one ever became accustomed to such a sight.

Gump Hoss slowed the wagon and stopped on the outskirts of the city. He and James sat very still, keeping their gaze forward. We heard shuffling footfalls, which stopped somewhere outside my line of vision.

"My God, James, what the hell happened to you out there?" a deep voice asked.

"Evening, Sheriff. We ran into Percival Templeton and his bunch. They claimed to be running an errand for

Pennyman," James replied. "We took exception."

"I wondered about the shotgun in your lap. I never knew either of you to go about armed like that." We heard movement, and a finger poked through one of the holes in the canvas. "This here looks like it wasn't a cordial conversation."

"It was...a spirited discussion," James countered.

"Banjo came in a little while ago, pulling your buggy behind him." The man moved away from the wagon. "He went straight to Fogg's Livery. John got him calmed down and taken care of. Your rig is a sight, I'll tell you," he reported.

"Yes, I imagine it is," James' tone was grim. "Sheriff, we need to talk. It's a long story. We're carrying women who have left the Pennyman ranch. I'll come to your office after we get them settled at Mrs. Dolan's."

"What women, James?" A note of cautious suspicion was in his voice. "Why did they come to town? Is anything amiss out there?"

"Let Gump Hoss and me get these ladies to Mrs. Dolan, and I'll tell you the whole sordid tale."

"You best do that. I'm sure you're gonna tell an interestin' story."

I heard the crunch of sand as the sheriff moved away from the wagon, and Gump Hoss urged the horses into a walk.

As James and Gump Hoss handed us down from the wagon bed in front of a large, whitewashed house, a woman opened the door and came down the steps. She stopped at the gate but came into the street upon espying Mrs. Hudson and Mrs. O'Malley.

The three women embraced and spoke in whispers before introducing Elizabeth, James, Gump Hoss, and me. Mrs. Dolan invited us inside. Gump Hoss declined, saying he would stay with the wagon and unload our baggage. The women, James, and I were soon comfortably seated in the drawing room.

Mrs. Dolan kept a private boardinghouse. All of the residents had been introduced to her by friends and acquaintances. Terms were agreed upon on a person-by-person basis.

Negotiations were soon completed, and accounts were reconciled by those requiring accommodation. After assisting Gump Hoss with the delivery of the luggage to our rooms, James bid us good night.

Believing none of us would see the grandfather again, we each took turns saying our goodbyes before Gump Hoss went off to stable the horses and seek his own lodgings.

Chapter 17

Despite extreme exhaustion, I laid awake with events of the past two days playing in my mind. As the first fingers of sunlight reached out to touch the earth, I abandoned all efforts of slumber to write in my journal. I moved the chair to the window in the early morning sunlight and watched the city awaken.

That day, starting so peacefully, became one of no little consternation for Mrs. Dolan's new boarders.

We met the other residents at breakfast. Mr. J.B. Mitchell and his son, Robert, had recently arrived in the city. Intent upon opening a hardware store, they ate quickly and left in search of a suitable building for their enterprise.

Mrs. Major Thurmond Young was recently widowed. Her husband had been an officer of the United States Army regiment occupying Corpus Christi and died in a mysterious manner.

Circumstances did not permit strict observance of the customary one year and one day mourning period, which the lady lamented to anyone so ill-fated as to engage in conversation with her. Mrs. Young and her daughter, Samantha, had been evicted from the comfortable house provided by the Army two days after the Major's funeral and installed in Mrs. Dolan's boardinghouse.

I learned that Samantha Young was an only child, I judged to be about sixteen years old. She habitually apologized for her mother's ill humor and rude remarks.

Fortunately for all under Mrs. Dolan's roof, Mrs. Young and her daughter would be returning to the East as soon as passage could be arranged.

Around four o'clock, James and Sheriff Henry W. Berry paid call. The sheriff asked to speak to the four of us together. With Mrs. Dolan's consent, he led us into the drawing room. We sat, expectantly watching the lawman as he assumed a stance in front of the fireplace. James stood by the closed door.

Presently, Sheriff Berry said, "James told me his version of what happened out on the road yesterday. I took a posse out at first light to look over the scene and bring in the bodies. They're over to the undertaker's waitin' burial."

We looked down at our laps as he stopped speaking. None of us responded.

"I gotta take your statements, ladies. Would you all wait in the hall or dining room until I call you in? Jane, I'll talk with you first," the older man added.

Mrs. Hudson remained seated as we rose. I looked down at her as we filed out of the room, offering a weak smile of encouragement. Impulsively, I reached out and lightly touched her shoulder. The housekeeper looked up at me with trepidation in her eyes as she grasped my fingertips. James remained inside and quietly shut the door after us.

Mrs. Hudson was in the drawing room for more than half an hour. She was somber and expressionless when she emerged from the interview. I noticed moisture on her cheeks as she quietly signaled Mrs. O'Malley it was her turn to talk with the lawman.

The door had scarcely closed when Mrs. O'Malley

returned to the hallway where Elizabeth and I waited our turn. She indicated I was the next to be questioned, speaking in an unusually clipped manner before she ascended the stairs.

I hesitated before entering the drawing room. Sheriff Berry appeared at the door and beckoned that I should enter.

I sat on the edge of an upholstered chair, hands folded on my lap, eyes averted to the floor. I wanted this interview concluded before the older man asked his first question.

"Miss Llewellyn," the sheriff began. "I don't mean to distress you, but I do need to know what happened to you yesterday."

"I understand, Sheriff," I said, not looking at the man. "I do not know where to start."

"Don't worry yourself, Miss. James told me about the doings out at the Huber farm. I need to hear the whole story from you."

"This matter started well before Mr. Kilpatrick took me to the Huber's," I said, wondering whether this man was trustworthy.

"James said as much but didn't elaborate. Said it wasn't his story to tell." Sheriff Berry leaned forward. "Problem is, what with you and Mrs. Owens being Yankees, Percival Templeton's death ain't sitting well with some folks."

"Mrs. Owens? Who's Mrs. Owens?" I asked. Realization dawning on me, I continued. "Do you mean Elizabeth? I didn't know she was married."

"Widowed, actually," the lawman advised. "All I'm sayin' is: you both need to stay out of sight until the dust settles."

"You should know, Sheriff, that I have no intention of staying in Texas any longer than necessary. I would leave today if there were an available conveyance." I could hear the bitterness in my voice.

"Well, you ain't goin' nowhere for near a fortnight. The stage won't be back till a week from Monday next. The mail packet left about an hour ago and won't be back for a week or ten days."

My heart sank at this news, but I looked straight at the sheriff as he brought the conversation back to the Butternut Man.

I told him all that had transpired from the time Templeton boarded the *Emma* in Corpus Christi Harbor until my return to the city the previous afternoon.

"Well, Miss, I do believe Judge Dix and Colonel Harris will be interested in your story. There's not much known about Josiah Pennyman or the goings-on at that ranch of his. The judge will hold court in Corpus Christi on Tuesday next. He might decide to order a formal inquest," Sheriff Berry informed me when I had finished.

I remained in the hall while Elizabeth was being questioned. I had difficulty sitting still and paced until I was certain I would wear a path in Mrs. Dolan's rug. After what seemed an eternity, the drawing room door opened, and Elizabeth slipped into the hall. She was pale and shaking. Her eyes were red. Tears stained her cheeks. She held a handkerchief to her mouth as she raced up the stairs without saying a word to anyone.

She had left the drawing room door open, and I went in, wanting to talk with the sheriff. "I trust you will not arrest Elizabeth before you talk with Judge Dix."

"I don't expect to arrest anyone for anything just yet. Do be mindful of the people around you if you go out. Mr. Templeton's friends are lying low for now, but they're going to want vengeance."

"Thank you, Sheriff. We will be cautious." I left the man standing in Mrs. Dolan's drawing room with his hat in his hands.

James followed me into the hall. He held out my carpetbag. "I found this still wedged under the buggy seat and figured you'd need it."

"Thank you," I murmured, taking the case. "You saved me a trip to town." I wanted to look in on Elizabeth and started up the stairs. Partway up, I turned and looked down at James. He was looking up at me, smiling.

"Please stay," I said. "I will put this in my room and come down."

He did not speak. I turned and went directly to my chamber. I set the carpetbag on the bed and opened it, mentally cataloging its contents.

I removed the clothing and toilet articles, setting them on the chiffonier. After closing and locking the carpetbag, I secreted it in a place I thought away from prying eyes and thieves and went to Elizabeth's room.

I knocked gently on the door, but there was no response. There were no sounds coming from within, giving rise to reason that either she had fallen asleep or was with Mrs. Hudson. I decided to look in on her later.

When I returned downstairs, I saw James standing at a window through the open drawing room door. There was no sign of the sheriff.

"How is Banjo?" I asked as I sat in the chair I had recently vacated.

"A bit worse for the wear, but he'll be fine. The buggy is a different matter. It's not a complete loss, but it will take quite a bit to put it to rights."

"I am sorry. I never should have involved you in my problems."

"I was already involved. Your father and Jacob Smythe

saw to that."

"Yes, I suppose so. Would you have time this afternoon to review those documents?"

"No, I have appointments the rest of the week. I'll have time Monday afternoon. Would you come to my office about two?"

"I shall be there." I suspected he was being untruthful about his schedule but was secretly grateful that I would not be required to leave the sanctuary of the house for some days.

"Good. Now, then, get some rest. This mess will be behind us soon." He made a shallow bow and started toward the door. "I'll let myself out."

I heard voices in the drawing room when I came downstairs for tea.

"You must turn out the murderess," Mrs. Young asserted.

"To whom are you referring?" Mrs. Dolan asked. Weariness tinged her words.

"Why, one of those young women I met at breakfast murdered two men yesterday afternoon," the widow reported. "As I heard the story, the woman kilt them for no good reason. They were out hunting, and she shot them dead from inside their wagon. It's beyond me why the sheriff hasn't clapped them all in irons." Mrs. Young's voice had become increasingly loud and shrill. She paced the room in evident agitation.

"You must not believe everything you hear in the shops," I interjected from the doorway.

"Was it you who kilt those men?" Mrs. Young spat, spinning around to face me.

"You ought not to speak of matters outside your ken," I

advised, amazed at the calmness in my voice.

The widow turned to Mrs. Dolan. "Tisn't right for respectable folk to associate with their sort. I demand you turn out those women."

"Do calm yourself, Mrs. Young," the proprietress implored. "From whom did you receive this information?"

"Billy Timmers was in Mr. Staple's store this morning telling anyone who would listen that a woman in a wagon kilt Patrick Higgins and Percival Templeton." Mrs. Young stood still, twisting her handkerchief until it was wound in a tight ball. She now stopped and pointed a finger at me. "Those people appeared here yesterday afternoon in a wagon, all dirty and disheveled. It doesn't take a Pinkerton detective to figure out one of those women is a murderess."

I wondered how to respond to this accusation and decided to remain mute.

"Neither of those men were pillars of society, Mrs. Young. I am sorry for Mrs. Higgins, though. I know what it is to lose someone you love." Mrs. Dolan picked up a miniature of a boy that sat on a table. There was a wistful look upon her countenance as she lightly touched the face of the image.

"Here I am, mourning the major, not yet cold in his grave," the widow sniffed dramatically and held her handkerchief to her face. "And you, Mrs. Dolan, harboring the murderess of another woman's husband. Well, I shan't associate with people who don't value life. My daughter and I shall keep to our room until those women have been expelled. See that our meals are brought to us." Mrs. Young rose and started toward the door, where I stood.

"Meals are served in the dining room," Mrs. Dolan sighed as she returned the miniature to its place, her eyes sparkling with unshed tears. "There will be no exceptions."

"Well, I never..." Mrs. Young could be heard continuing

her diatribe as she took the stairs to the second floor.

"Thank you, Mrs. Dolan," I began.

"Jane Hudson told me about the incident on the road," she said. "You must excuse Mrs. Young. She is a troubled soul."

"Assuredly. I am certain we can find other, more pleasant topics of conversation," I said as I settled on the horsehair divan.

We engaged in small talk while others drifted into the room.

The newspaper account of the embroilment on the road was factual. The report told of an ambush but was vague as to who ambushed whom. It was expected that the article would give rise to rumors. We were not disappointed.

Mrs. Young could be depended upon to repeat the most outrageous and gruesome stories over meals while maintaining her belief that all four of us would kill again. She expressed her disappointment that she would not be present for the trial and hanging of a murderess in Corpus Christi.

Mrs. Dolan was visibly upset by all the talk of shootings and death. She became pale and shook from the top of her head to the tips of her shoes. She appeared to be fighting back tears and refused to contribute to the conversation. She usually found a reason to absent herself from the room whenever the topic arose but never stopped anyone from speaking their mind on the subject.

Over dinner Thursday afternoon, Mr. Mitchell informed us that Patrick Higgins had been buried.

Mrs. Young enquired about Mr. Templeton's interment

and received only withering looks from round the table for her trouble. She then murmured something about paying a condolence call on Patrick Higgins' widow.

Chapter 18

Two o'clock Monday afternoon found me sitting across from James Kilpatrick in his office. He sat behind a large desk covered with papers and stacks of files, looking very imposing.

"Would you be able to assist me in making inquiries into securing a teaching position?" I asked.

"Do you believe your situation so wretched that you must seek employment, Miss Llewellyn?" His face was masterfully blank, displaying neither emotion nor information.

"My father has abandoned me. I have neither brother nor husband. To my knowledge, I have no other living relation. Without anyone to support me, the logical conclusion is that I shall have to support myself. I must conserve what little funds I have remaining. Therefore, I must infer that I shall have to engage in an occupation for which I am suited."

"Would your mind be put at ease if I informed you that you shall not be required to toil for your bread?" A small smile played at the corner of his mouth.

"How can that be?" I am sure the puzzlement I felt showed on my face.

James chuckled as he picked up a document from the top of a sheaf of papers in front of him and handed it to me. "Your father established a trust from which you shall receive an annual income."

"I see," I responded, cautiously taking the document and briefly scanning the first page. "Is this income predicated upon marriage?"

"No. It seems he anticipated your refusal to wed Mr. Pennyman." The attorney next selected a small envelope and set it on the desk in front of me. "Matron or spinster, the stipend is yours."

I took the envelope. Father's careful script in the familiar blue ink gave me pause. I looked at James. "Josiah thinks me a pauper, and this is a very small community. I am informed that the stagecoach shall return in a week's time. I must make certain transactions prior to the journey. People will surely take notice. I have seen how fast news of any sort travels through this community. One cannot sneeze without the entire populous knowing of it within the hour."

"That long?" he laughed. "You and I are the only two who know. I assure you, what is spoken in this office will remain between the two of us. I shall see to Mrs. Owen's comfort in the anti-room while you read that." He gestured toward the letter as he got up and left the room, closing the door behind him.

I had little knowledge of Papa's business practices or his financial status. He had always been well respected in Norwich. I opened the envelope and read the letter. Twice.

In 1862, Papa and Josiah Pennyman opened a factory and had been awarded government contracts to manufacture leather cartridge belts and pouches for the United States Army and Navy. They had employed more than a hundred men and women.

Although the factory was near Norwich, a man was hired to superintend the workers. Father did not involve himself in the daily management of the business but received regular reports and copies of contracts for the goods they manufactured.

Josiah was traveling when General Lee surrendered. The government contracts expired the following month and were not renewed. Father dispatched his attorney and accountant to the factory to gather the files and bookkeeping materials for audit before final disbursements to the partners. He also sent instructions to the factory manager to discharge the employees with two week's wages. The equipment and remaining raw materials were to be sold.

In the course of conducting the audit, Mr. Forsythe, the accountant, discovered that Josiah's man had been keeping two sets of books. The factory manager and bookkeeper had been careless and left behind letters, invoices, and other documents showing sales to the Confederate government.

When Josiah learned that the factory had been shuttered, he was furious and came to Norwich to confront Father. He insisted manufacturing must be resumed, adamant there was a civilian market for their goods, though no one seemed to know who, other than the military, would have any use for such items.

The cattleman was beyond reasoning. But, everything had been sold. Pennyman demanded immediate payment of his share, including all the funds generated by the illicit contracts.

Papa refused, stating that there were payments due from the government for the last two shipments, and he was not willing to overlook the illegal sales. He wanted a full accounting. Papa informed Josiah that copies of the audit would be sent to him in Corpus Christi with his final payment—in gold.

The Texas rancher eventually acquiesced to Papa's way of thinking. Josiah went away, seemingly satisfied with the resolution. Some days later, Papa received a letter. A copy was enclosed.

November 15, 1865

Mr. Llewellyn,

Having time to consider our most recent conversation, I have determined that the terms for the dissolution of our partnership are disagreeable and shall not stand. That you should reap any benefit from my special customers is repugnant to me and shall not be tolerated.

The resolution to this matter is one that I believe will be mutually beneficial. In addition to the gold you promised to send me, I shall take your daughter to wife. If she has not arrived in Corpus Christi, Texas, by the end of May 1866, I shall send my agents to escort her.

Do not design to trick me. The consequence of refusing this proposal shall be dire for you, indeed.

Your son-in-law,
Josiah Pennyman

I rose from the chair and paced about the room, trembling with rage. I was surprised that no tears sprang forth. For once, my eyes were dry.

The pages were crushed in my left hand as I stood at the window of the small office. I did not hear James open the door and come into the room. I was vaguely aware of the clink of china as he placed a tray on the edge of his desk and came to stand behind me.

"How could he have done such a thing?" I asked.

"Your father thought they were engaged in a legitimate business venture," he responded in a hushed voice.

"How could Papa agree to Josiah's demands?" I turned around and looked up at James, raising the crumpled letters to his eye. The volume of my voice rose as I spoke. "He went to Africa to help the Negros, and gave his daughter as payment for dissolution of a business." The longer I spoke, the angrier I became. I sank into a chair and glowered at the pages in my hand. Softly, I asked, "Why would he want to share in ill-gotten gain? I cannot make sense of any of this." I stood and thrust the letters at the attorney. "Here, read for yourself. I am sickened with the knowledge that *my father* is a coward."

He backed away, allowing the sheets of paper to fall to the floor. "I received letters of my own," he admitted as he guided me to a chair and seated himself behind the desk. "The Michael Llewellyn I knew was an honest man and expected others to be the same. By the time he learned of the illicit sales and realized his name could be connected to them, he had unwittingly closed down the enterprise.

"I made some inquiries and am satisfied that the facts, as your father states them, are true. I have an appointment to talk with Colonel Harris, commander of the occupying troops. He is in a better position to determine the best course to take."

"Did my father go to Africa to avoid going to prison?"

"I don't know. As far as I have been able to ascertain, he did not know about the contracts with the Confederates until after the factory was closed. I am told that their manufacturing practices were excellent. It has been alleged that they were overcharging the government, but they weren't the only business doing that, and they did have signed contracts with the War Department." James had been thumbing through the stack of papers as he spoke. He stopped talking to look at a sheet he pulled from it. "All of this is hearsay. I have no first-hand knowledge of any of this."

"I am more confused now than I was during all those weeks on the *Emma*," I whispered, closing my eyes and shaking my head.

"I'm afraid your departure from our fair city may be delayed. Colonel Harris will want to talk with you.

"If this matter cannot be settled in a week's time, then it must be so."

We sat quietly for some moments as I pondered my new situation. "Do I have immediate access to the funds in these bank accounts?"

"Yes, of course. Why do you ask?"

"I would like to compensate the Hubers for the damage done to their farm. They were so very kind to open their home to me, and it brought evil and destruction to their doorstep. Perhaps I can pay for the reconstruction of their fencing or purchase replacement livestock?"

"I'm sure Otto and Ute would appreciate the gift. I'll make the arrangements for you."

"I'll write a note to be sent with the money this evening." That being settled, I moved on to another thought. "Have you spoken with Gump Hoss, or did he already return to the ranch?"

"He wasn't in any hurry to get back. He wanted to replace the shot-up stave on the wagon. And he had a long list of supplies that would have taken a day or two to put together. I'm not sure whether he's still in town or has returned to the ranch."

"That's good. A few days rest would have given that draft horse some time to heal before he had to pull that heavy load." I took the liberty of pouring myself another cup of tea and looked over the cup. After taking a sip, I asked, "How long will it take to repair your buggy?"

"The saddler says he has to order the leather for the seat. He didn't have enough oilcloth on hand to make the new bonnet, either. But, the blacksmith was able to put the wheel back on properly."

"Can both of these men be found at the livery stable?"

"Uh, yes, I suppose. Why?"

"I'd like to pay for those repairs, as well. There's no reason for that to come out of your pocket."

"That's not necessary, Priscilla. I might not have a huge income, but I have enough to see to my expenses."

"I'm not questioning that. I feel responsible for the troubles visited upon you and the Hubers. Since my father has seen to it that I have these funds, I prefer to use it for good. If I can ease some of the Hubers' burden, as well as your own, I plan to do just that."

"That's an interesting way of putting it." He stopped a moment, his face a study of concentration. "Thank you. It is most generous of you."

"Then, it's settled. I'll go to the stable and settle with the saddler and blacksmith."

Before our meeting concluded, we discussed the contents of the parcel Jacob Smythe had left. James agreed to accompany me to the warehouse to inventory my possessions.

As Elizabeth and I left the law office, I wondered if I would ever be able to shake the dust of Corpus Christi, Texas, from my boots.

Elizabeth and I sat at a small table in a corner of the restaurant of the Union House Hotel. A plate of pastries and a pot of tea sat on the table between us.

"I did not know you were married until last week when the sheriff questioned us," I said, picking up the teapot and pouring out.

"My husband died in a mining accident in California nearly two years ago," she replied, her eyes downcast as she unfolded a napkin.

"How is it you came to be in Texas?" I coaxed.

"Horace spent three years in the Army. There were men from California in his regiment, and they talked about the gold. After he mustered out, he was restless and went to California to seek his fortune. He had a modicum of success in the goldfields and sent for me. He was killed in a mining accident while I was still at sea." Elizabeth spoke softly, with little inflection. She selected a pastry and placed it on the plate in front of her.

"Oh, Elizabeth, I am so sorry."

"Thank you, Priscilla. He was a good man, except when he took to the drink. He was malevolent when he drank, which wasn't all that often, and he was always repentant afterward."

"Did he strike you?" The memory of Crenshaw's demented face, the odor of his breath and person, his hands pawing at my clothes, the ship's noises, and the horror of that stormy night on the *Emma* came flooding into my mind. I forced it out to concentrate on the woman who sat across from me, the sorrow on her face, and the soft words she spoke.

"He blackened my eyes a few times, tore out some hair, and left bruises all over, but he never broke any bones.

Horace was a good man, and I loved him. I still love him."

The tea and dainties lay forgotten as Elizabeth's expression took on a glazed appearance, her eyes unfocused and her mouth drawn taut. She stared straight ahead, her face void of expression as though she was seeing her husband in her mind's eye.

"His mining partner met the ship and told me about the accident," she continued. "He bought Horace's share of the mine and assisted with other legal matters." Her voice became wistful. "And then he was gone, back to his mine. I was alone and didn't know a soul in San Francisco."

She shook her head and looked across the table at me, smiling weakly. "I wanted to see more of the West before I returned home. I became acquainted with a family in San Francisco. Down on their luck, they decided to move to Texas. The missus said she was sickly and wouldn't be able to tend their three children during the journey. They asked whether I would consider taking the position, and I accepted."

Elizabeth's expression became stony as she remembered. "The woman didn't budge from her bed in the wagon the whole trip, even when we stopped for the night. I shan't speak further of her." She sighed, and her face softened. "The children were delightful, and we got along famously.

"We hadn't been in Corpus Christi an hour when the woman miraculously recovered from her imaginary ailment. A half-hour after that, she was chatting up the gents of the town." That far-away expression had vanished. She picked up a knife and fork and commenced cutting the pastry. "They opened a tavern. I heard they employ soiled doves." She sighed and took a sip of her tea.

"After I received my wages, I took a room in a respectable boardinghouse and began looking for work suitable for a decent Christian woman."

"I was in Mr. Staple's store one afternoon when I saw a notice that Mr. Pennyman was in need of a housemaid. I made enquiries and accepted the position when it was offered to me. He appeared to be a gentleman, though I should have been suspicious of his character when I saw the name he gave his ranch." She slowly shook her head. "Still, he never bothered me and paid regular as clockwork—in gold."

I thought about what she told me and asked, "What are your plans, Elizabeth?"

"My husband is buried near his mine in California. I've never even seen his grave. I have no family hereabouts. I shall go home. I have quite a large family, and I miss them."

"Where is home?"

"Pennsylvania. My father has a farm between Gettysburg and Cashtown. My uncles and cousins are nearby in Gettysburg."

"I envy you your family. My father is my only living relation and is on the other side of the world."

As Elizabeth poured tea into her cup, she asked, "Was there anyone for you before Mr. Pennyman?"

I closed my eyes, certain the pain of recalling Ethen Brandt showed on my face. "Yes," I murmured and squared my shoulders. "One of my closest friends had a cousin the same age as her brother.

"Ethan and I met at the Independence Day picnic in 1860. Papa gave his permission for Ethan to court me on New Year's Eve. He was in his final year at Yale when President Lincoln declared war on the Confederates. He and his cousin, Philip, enlisted in the Connecticut Volunteers. We wrote, and I sent packages.

"In January 1864, Ethan and Philip received thirty days

furlough after signing reenlistment papers at the end of their three years. It was glorious to have him home. We became engaged and planned to marry before he returned to the Fifth Connecticut Infantry.

"I started thinking about Anne, a friend whose husband was in the cavalry. Her father forced her out of her home and tried to take her child. Ethan's uncle helped her.

"I don't believe Papa would ever behave in that manner, but I didn't want to live alone. Nor did I want to live with my father on his farm after I was a married woman.

"Ethan and I took long walks and discussed my concerns. We agreed we would wait to wed until after he was mustered out of the infantry."

Elizabeth reached out and placed her hand atop her friend's, but remained silent.

"Then, on the sixteenth of March in 1865, Ethan was at Silver Run, North Carolina. He was shot and killed. Philip told me he was buried under a tree near the battlefield."

Elizabeth was silent for a bit. She pushed the pastry around her plate, cut off a piece with a fork, ate it, and sipped her tea. She looked at me, a smile growing across her face. "Come with me." The tone of her voice and the warmth in her eyes encouraged me.

"Where?" I asked, startled out of my reverie.

"To Pennsylvania. We can secure housing together. I've been on my own too long and don't want to live under my father's roof, either." The excitement of the idea was visible on Elizabeth's face and in her eyes.

I considered this proposal. There was nothing for me in Connecticut, and I certainly did not want to stay in Texas. While on the *Emma*, I realized I wanted to be my own person. Though, now that it was within my grasp, I was wary of it.

To be my own person, to establish my own home, to be

able to decide and dictate my own future was daunting and exhilarating and frightening. "I should love to travel to Pennsylvania with you," I heard myself say.

After paying for the tea, we went to Mr. Staples' store. With our lists in hand, we entered the mercantile to find every clerk dashing about, looking at items, calling out prices, and writing quickly.

An elderly man stood at the counter, holding a small mutilated stick. The customer was running a finger down the stick as he enumerated the purchases apparently represented by the notches cut in it, "...terbacce, twinty-five; ax for John, seventy-five; one tin washpot for the old woman, two-thirty; one darr; two gallons whiskey for Auld Jerry's wake..." and so on to the end of the stick.

The bustling clerks slowed, and a report given to the customer. Finally satisfied that he was being charged correctly, the old man settled his account and turned on his heel. He walked away from the counter, tossed the scarred stick on the wood pile next to the stove, and left the store.

"I beg pardon for the ballyhoo, ladies," said a man from behind the counter, mopping his brow with his handkerchief. "How may I help you today?"

"I'd like to look at your buttons, if I may," Elizabeth requested.

The clerk turned, brought down a shallow basket from a shelf behind him, and placed it on the counter. "This is all we have right now. We expect a shipment of buttons from the East on the next boat from Indianola."

Elizabeth began looking through the button cards, setting aside several for further inspection.

The clerk turned to me. "And, for you, Miss?"

I handed him my list. He moved about efficiently, selecting items from shelves and placing them on the counter. When he had ticked off the last item, he asked, "Will there be anything else, Miss?"

"No, that is all for today. Thank you," I replied.

He removed a pencil from behind his right ear, wrote down each selection and its price, and added the column of numbers. "That'll be a dollar and two bits, Miss."

I withdrew coins from my reticule and placed them on the counter.

The man looked at me, a peculiar expression crossed his face as he put his hand over the money. "Ain't you the woman come to marry Mr. Pennyman?"

The question startled me. *Was he one of Templeton's men?* I decided it best to be truthful. "Yes."

The clerk leaned over the counter, eyes narrowed, face darkening, and teeth bared, "Mr. Pennyman is comin' for you." His voice was low and menacing. He brought himself upright. A genial smile returned, along with his natural coloring. After wrapping my purchases and pushing the parcel toward me, he went to assist Elizabeth.

I stood with my hand on the package, staring at the clerk, shaken by his utterance. The promise to remain in Corpus Christi made to James Kilpatrick less than two hours past weighed heavily upon me. *Would I never be safe?* My greatest desire was to book passage on the first transport away from this inhospitable city.

I took several deep breaths to calm myself and watched Elizabeth engaged in conversation with the clerk.

"What did the clerk say to you?" Elizabeth asked as soon as we were outside the store. "You look as though you've seen a ghost."

Still shaken by the clerk's statement, I did not immediately respond but walked with purpose as we crossed the street. We stepped onto the wooden walkway in front of a row of shops. I looked at Elizabeth and stammered, "I...I need to think. We should return to Mrs. Dolan's. Supper will be served soon."

Whether Judge Dix would order a formal inquest had been hotly debated for the past week. So, there was great interest in what Sheriff Berry had to say when he called at the boardinghouse Tuesday afternoon. The dinner was postponed as the entire household crowded into the little drawing room.

Sitting on a wooden chair brought in from the dining room, his hat on his knee, the sheriff glanced around the room before speaking.

"Why haven't you arrested anyone for those murders?" Mrs. Young demanded.

"Because it weren't murder," the sheriff replied. "I wanted to talk to these women in private. But it's gonna be public knowledge soon enough. If you have no objection, ladies, I might as well say what I got to say to everyone." He looked directly at Elizabeth.

"I have no objection, sir," the former maid stated. Mrs. Hudson, Mrs. O'Malley, and I nodded agreement.

"I just come from a meeting with Judge Dix, Colonel Harris, and Mayor Staples. I told them what Mr. Kilpatrick, Gump Ho . . . ah, Mr. Thompson, Billy Timmers, Leland Jones, and you four ladies had to say about the altercation last week. I also told them what the boys and I saw when we went out to bring the bodies back to town.

“It was agreed that there ain’t no call for a formal inquest. No one’s gonna be charged with murder, neither. They was protecting you all and your property. We don’t see that Mr. Thompson and Mrs. Owens had any other recourse but to shoot those two men.”

“But, but...” Mrs. Young sputtered and fell silent when everyone in the room turned to look at her.

Samantha blushed and shot a glance at Robert Mitchell, who rolled his eyes.

“Mrs. Young, there ain’t no reason to carry on so. Your ranting is just raisin’ more of a ruckus all over town. Mrs. Owens done what she had to do. That’s all there is to it,” the lawman sternly explained and turned to Mrs. Dolan. “Thank you for your hospitality, ma’am. I’ll see myself out.”

The sheriff left the room, and I heard the door shut behind him. The silence was broken only by the ticking of the tall clock in the corner.

Later that evening, as we were sitting down to supper, Mr. Mitchell discretely passed a folded sheet of foolscap to me. The handwriting was an unfamiliar scrawl with widely spaced letters and the subtlest slant to the right. A quick glance at the signature reassured me, and I quickly read the missive, consisting of just one line:

Urgent that you come to my office tomorrow morning at ten o’clock.

James Kilpatrick, Esq.

I thanked Mr. Mitchell for his messenger services, tucked the paper into the sleeve of my dress, and took my place at the table.

Mrs. Young had been inobtrusive since Sheriff Berry's announcement. She glared at Elizabeth but said nothing until after thanks had been offered to the Almighty for the repast set before us.

"You must be pleased, Mrs. Owens," the widow remarked, passing the tureen filled with stew to Samantha.

"And why would that be?" Elizabeth countered.

"You shan't be prosecuted for murdering that man. Percival Templeton, wasn't it? Or, did you shoot Patrick Higgins?"

"I believe the sheriff put this matter to rest, Madam," Mr. Mitchell interjected. "Do desist excoriating the woman further. There's been too much talk of this beastly affair."

"I fail to understand your eagerness to see me hanged," Elizabeth said, looking the widow full in the face.

"Someone needs to pay for the spilling of innocent blood." Mrs. Young enunciated each word carefully.

"Innocent?" Mr. Mitchell exclaimed. "Neither of those men were innocents. They both were known for behaviors not spoken of in polite society."

"I believe Billy Timmers. He says they were out for a day of hunting. Those men meant y'all no harm," Mrs. Young's speech slipped into the gentle lilting of Southern speech patterns.

"Madam," Mr. Mitchell began slowly. "Are you Southern-born?"

"Of course I am," she replied, sitting a little taller.

"Well, that explains it," Mrs. Hudson said under her breath. Then, addressing the woman directly, "Had you been as well acquainted with Mr. Templeton as I was, you would know he was no gentleman, Southern or otherwise."

Mrs. Young, her face contorted in hatred, and fire in her eyes, turned to look at the older woman, "How dare you address me? I cannot imagine why Mrs. Dolan allows you to dine with the paying boarders. Where I come from, servants take their meals in the kitchen."

Everyone at the table was stunned by the insult. Discomfort descended upon the room. I looked at my plate, embarrassed for the widow. It was Mrs. Dolan who lashed out.

"Mrs. Young, I would thank you to keep a civil tongue in your head and mind your own affairs, not mine or those of the people at this table. Who pays for the privilege of living under this roof is mine to determine." She set down the empty bowl she'd been holding and put her hands on her hips. "I have been acquainted with Mrs. Hudson and Mrs. O'Malley many years. I am proud to count them as friends. Their husbands, God rest their souls, were respected businessmen in this city long before you knew Corpus Christi existed. These women have known the sorrow of losing their husbands and homes.

"They went into service for Mr. Pennyman because there is little work for decent women hereabouts. He was new in town. Nothing was known of the man's character. They are not responsible for his lack of social graces, nor are they responsible for the actions of a band of gullible men doing the bidding of a wealthy landowner.

"Should you be unable to remain civil when speaking to my friends and boarders, I shall ask Colonel Harris to remove you from these premises."

Everyone at the table exchanged glances, uncertain how to respond to our landlady's outburst. I suppressed the urge to stand and applaud and instead concealed a smile behind my napkin.

Mr. Mitchell was not so discrete. He smiled broadly, nodding toward Mrs. Dolan in agreement with her sentiments.

Mouth agape and face flushed, Mrs. Young stood, allowing the napkin she had placed on her lap to fall to the floor. "Well, I never. How dare you," she sputtered. "Come, Samantha. These people are not fit company."

"I should like to finish my meal, Mother." The girl kept her eyes trained on her plate.

"So, they've turned you against me, as well. I might have known. I've observed how you look at this...this boy. I demand that you come upstairs with me." She moved toward the door. "Now."

"I am no longer a child to be ordered about, Mother." The girl's voice remained calm and soft. "I am a woman of sixteen. I shall come up when I have finished my meal."

The whole of the household sat in stunned silence during the exchange. Mrs. Young stalked from the room, her face crimson with anger.

As the sound of the woman's footfalls on the stairs receded, I reflected on Samantha's defiance and stole glances at her and Robert. The boy was blushing and grinning from ear to ear.

"I apologize for my mother," Samantha said just above a whisper, her eyes still downcast.

Mr. Mitchell leaned toward her, a kind expression on his face. "You needn't apologize for her. She has endured many hardships of late."

The girl looked up at him, gratitude writ on her face. "Thank you for your kindness, Mr. Mitchell. She is always in ill-temper, always finding fault or looking at a thing in the worst possible light. I cannot recall her enjoying a single moment of happiness. My poor father…" The girl had cleaned her plate and touched the napkin to her mouth. "Thank you, Mrs. Dolan. The beef stew was delicious. Excuse me, please." Placing the napkin on the table beside her plate, she rose, tucked in the chair, and left the dining room.

We ate in silence. I wondered what had transpired in her life to cause Mrs. Young to be so disagreeable.

The scent of strong tea filled James Kilpatrick's office as he poured out and handed a cup and saucer to me. He sat in the chair adjacent to mine rather than behind his desk.

"I spoke with Colonel Harris yesterday afternoon. The colonel has asked to speak with you about your time at Gehenna. Would you be up to that meeting today? Now?"

"Yes. I think so," I said, uncertainty shadowing my words as I sipped the hot, fragrant brew.

"Good. Wait here. I'll be right back." The attorney rose from his chair and was out the door in two strides. I heard the murmur of voices. A pungent cigar odor preceded the Army officer as he passed through the doorway to stand in front of the chair recently vacated by the attorney.

James made the introductions and took his place behind the desk. The colonel turned his chair toward me and sat. Leaning forward, he started to ask his questions.

Colonel Harris, James, and I spoke for more than two hours as the story of my voyage on the *Emma* and the days spent at Gehenna was related. The colonel requested that I remain in Corpus Christi a while longer. I hesitated, not certain how to respond, and told them about the clerk at Mr. Staple's store.

Neither man had an explanation for the clerk's odd

behavior or statement. Josiah was not expected for another six weeks. Colonel Harris wanted to post an armed guard at the boardinghouse, which I adamantly opposed. I intended to honor Mrs. Dolan's prohibition of firearms on her property. Mrs. Hudson had disclosed that the landlady's son had been shot and killed with his own rifle, which she had given him on his sixteenth birthday.

The two gentlemen were resolute. After a long debate, they conceded there would be no guard, armed or otherwise. In return, I agreed to remain in Corpus Christi for no more than a fortnight to consult with them as they worked out what would be done regarding Josiah Pennyman and what if any, charges would be brought against him.

Thursday morning, James called, and we set off for the warehouse where Jacob Smythe had deposited my possessions. The warehouse was on a street near the docks, in a most unsavory neighborhood. The stench of fish, rotting food, stale spirits, and human waste was overpowering. I sent up a silent prayer that I wouldn't become ill in public and thus embarrass either of us.

After showing the watchman the documents Jacob had left for me, we easily gained access to my goods, and I looked through the boxes and cases that had been neatly stacked on a low shelf in the middle of a long aisle.

Finding everything in order and discovering a few items I had thought lost to me, I redistributed my possessions within the boxes to free up one to transport the found treasures. We assured ourselves that the remaining boxes were secured and left the warehouse.

James tucked the small box of possessions under one arm and offered the other to me as we wound through the streets and returned to Mrs. Dolan's.

As he set the box on a table in the foyer, Mrs. Dolan invited him to sit in the drawing room and have a glass of lemonade. After being under the warming sun, it was nice to be sitting in the cool room.

"James, would it be an imposition to ask you to see that those boxes in the warehouse were sent to me when I'm settled?" I asked.

"You sure you don't want to take them with you?" he countered.

I pondered this question before responding. "If I leave by stagecoach, there won't be space for everything. Since I don't know by which conveyance I'll be traveling, I'm planning for all contingencies."

"Point well taken. In that case, yes, I'll be pleased to carry out that service for you." He pulled his watch from its pocket in his vest and looked at it. "I have an appointment in about an hour. I must get back to my office. Good day, Priscilla."

"Good day. Thank you for escorting me to the warehouse."

I walked with him to the door and watched as he made his way down the walk, through the gate, and started down the street before shutting the door.

The next three days progressed slowly. With little to do and nowhere to go, the days were long, though not lonely.

The Confederate loyalists were dissatisfied that no one would hang for the Butternut Man's death. They held rallies and talked of coming for Elizabeth. I believed her to be in greater danger of physical harm than I.

sMrs. Young surceased in her diatribe but took to lurking

about the house. She peered around corners and stood in deep shadows, watching the household go about their daily routines. She left the house every afternoon after dinner and returned promptly at six.

Mrs. Hudson, Mrs. O'Malley, Elizabeth, and I kept to ourselves, as much to avoid Mrs. Young as to support one another during this difficult time. We took turns reading aloud from my small library while mending or sewing or engaging in some other form of needlework. We talked at length about our futures, where we should go, and what we should do.

At long last, Monday arrived. There was a time of arrival printed in the stagecoach timetable, but it was common knowledge that the conveyance was routinely two hours late. Nonetheless, Mrs. Dolan insisted that Mrs. Young be at the stop in front of the Union House Hotel at the published hour. The widow and her daughter were in a frenzy of activity as they packed the last of their belongings and searched every room for items perceived to be missing.

At the appointed hour, a dashing young officer appeared at the boardinghouse. He introduced himself as Lieutenant Jordan Grayson and announced that he had been given the honor of escorting Mrs. Major Thurmond Young and Miss Young to the stagecoach.

He consigned their luggage to a sergeant, who looked as though he ought to still be in knee-breeches. The sergeant, in turn, ordered a Negro private to load the cases onto a handcart and take them to the stagecoach stop. The lieutenant then proffered his arm to the widow while a corporal escorted Miss Young. They left the boardinghouse, following the cart tracks. No farewells were offered by anyone.

The tension, so prevalent during the past two weeks, left with the widow, and peace reigned over Mrs. Dolan's boardinghouse.

We had just sat down to dinner when there was a rap on the door. Mrs. Dolan went to answer it. We heard her exclaim and the murmur of voices. Our landlady returned, followed by Samantha Young.

Robert Mitchell jumped up, upsetting his chair, which clattered to the floor. He rushed to her and embraced her. Then, remembering himself, he blushed, escorted her to a place at the table, and uprighted his chair.

While Mrs. Dolan rushed about to set a place for the young lady, Mrs. Hudson asked, "Is your mother returning as well?"

"No. Mother was fuming, but I saw her onto the stagecoach and watched it leave. She's on her way to Brownsville." The young woman looked at Robert with adoring eyes.

Mr. Mitchell had been attempting a look of disapproval but failed and asked in a resigned voice, "When shall we have the banns read?"

"I wanted to tell you, Father, but..." Words failed Robert Mitchell. He looked from his father to Samantha and back again, unable to utter a syllable.

"We would like them read as soon as possible," Samantha replied. The girl was radiant.

Mrs. Dolan reappeared with a place setting. As we began serving ourselves, Samantha told her story.

"Well, you all know how our morning started. Mother was in high spirits and talked the entire distance to the stage stop. The lieutenant listened politely and even laughed with her. Corporal Mark Benning and I followed. I danced with the corporal at my cotillion in April, and he had been very nice. I asked him to hold back my luggage that I did not intend to accompany my mother on her journey." A coquettish expression crossed her countenance. "He was reluctant to do as I asked, but I was able to persuade him."

"Should I be worried about this Corporal Benning?" Robert asked, a mischievous glint in his eyes.

"Not at all," Samantha said, reaching for the water pitcher. "His enlistment will be up in a few weeks, and he'll be returning to his home in Missouri.

"Mark talked to the Negro private and had him set aside my bags. Mother was so engrossed in talking to Lieutenant Grayson that she completely ignored the activity around her. I stayed near Mother but not at her side. As more people came, I just kept moving back to the edge of the crowd.

"When the stagecoach arrived, I stayed with my back against the hotel wall, under the porch cover, until everyone had boarded and the driver shut the door. Mother realized I was not on board about the time the horses started walking. She did not have a window and had to lean over a portly gentleman, who was not amused with her forwardness. He began a diatribe that quite drowned out hers. I stood on the walk and waved her goodbye." The girl sat back in her chair with a self-satisfied expression. "Corporal Bening escorted me here."

As I looked about at the faces at the table, I saw smiles and shaking shoulders, as though the people were enjoying the picture of someone behaving more boorishly than Mrs. Young.

We sat at the table, talking of the betrothal of Samantha and Robert long after the meal had been consumed. It was a very pleasant afternoon.

Mrs. Hudson, having previously owned a restaurant, and Mrs. O'Malley, having previously owned an inn and tavern with her late husband, conspired to combine their knowledge and open a tea shop. Neither was enamored with Corpus Christi, and Mr. Kilpatrick assisted them in making arrangements to take passage on a merchant ship to Indianola, where they would hire a conveyance to carry them to Austin two days after Mrs. Young had departed.

We walked with them to the dock, where the lighter was waiting to take them to the ship. We all embraced and cried, lamenting the loss of society of ones who had become dear to us.

The house was even quieter without the two older women, though Samantha and Robert kept up a lively conversation during meals. I looked forward to receiving correspondence from the former servants after they were settled in their new situation.

Elizabeth was anxious to leave but understood the obligation I had to James and Colonel Harris. I promised her that I would conclude my business as quickly as possible that we might book our passage, as well.

James Kilpatrick came to visit regularly, sometimes staying for supper. Mr. Mitchell and he discovered they had much in common and spent many hours in the drawing room talking and playing chess.

Mr. Mitchell and Robert found their building and began stocking the shelves of their hardware store. Mrs. Mitchell was expected to arrive within the month. The family would then begin their search for a home of their own. The wedding would take place after Robert's mother arrived.

Colonel Harris asked to speak with me again, to which I consented. James called for me, and we walked to the military headquarters Wednesday morning.

The colonel was pleasant but stern. He asked me again to relate what I knew of Josiah Pennyman's history when we met and what we talked about.

I did my best to assure the officer that I never laid eyes on Josiah Pennyman in Connecticut and that I met him for the first time when I arrived at Gehenna.

An hour later, Colonel Harris was satisfied that I would be of no use in whatever legal proceedings may eventually ensue. The colonel granted permission for me to leave Corpus Christi and the state of Texas.

I returned to the boardinghouse in a state of giddiness. Mrs. Dolan and Elizabeth were in the dining room when James and I came into the house, talking gaily.

"My, you're in high spirits. If I didn't know you as well as I do, I'd suspect you of imbibing," Elizabeth declared, looking up from the coverlet she and Mrs. Dolan were quilting.

"Oh, yes, my dear friend," I exclaimed, dancing around the room. "The best news possible: I have been given permission to leave Texas."

"I shall dislike your leaving," Mrs. Dolan said, keeping her eyes on her stitchery. "But that is the way of boardinghouses. Folks come and go."

"We aren't gone yet," Elizabeth said. "I'm sure we shall be here a while longer. It may be weeks before a ship comes in that will be going to the East."

"Shall I look into shipping schedules?" James interjected. "The wharf is no place for ladies."

"Yes, thank you," I said, sobering a little. "Perhaps we could sail to Indianola and travel to Austin. I would like to see Mrs. Hudson and Mrs. O'Malley once more."

"I should like that, as well," Elizabeth agreed.

"I shall be off to the wharf, then," Mr. Kilpatrick said. "I bid you, ladies, adieu."

We heard the door close. Elizabeth and I looked at each other, giggling like schoolgirls.

James returned the next morning. He removed a paper from his pocket, upon which was a handwritten list of ships sailing to Indianola and their anticipated departure dates.

"It seems you will be able to leave as early as tomorrow morning," he informed us.

"Oh, that is much too soon," Elizabeth exclaimed.

"There is another sailing on Tuesday next," he said, pointing to a line on the page.

"That is fine with me," I mused, looking to Elizabeth for her answer. I could scarcely believe we were escaping this oppressive city.

"Yes, that would be perfect," she said.

"Then, I shall book passage for you on the *Lorena*." He folded the paper and restored it to his pocket as the tall clock chimed the hour. "Good heavens, is it really ten o'clock? I'm late for an appointment. I shall call on you this evening." He rushed out of the house, shutting the door a little harder than necessary.

Elizabeth and I went upstairs to commence packing.

Chapter 19

The days flew by as we did laundry and packed our trunks and bags. There were sundries I wanted to purchase. Elizabeth and I agreed we would do our shopping the day before the ship was scheduled to sail.

We left the boardinghouse shortly after breakfast on Monday morning, intent on returning before the heat of the day was upon us. We went to Mr. Staple's store to purchase toothpowder, knitting wool, and a few other items. I was relieved to look around and see the clerk who had previously waited on us was not behind the counter. Our purchases were made without trouble or fanfare. Having spent less time shopping than anticipated, Elizabeth and I decided to treat ourselves to pastries at the Union House Hotel.

We were led to a table near the middle of the restaurant, settled our parcels and ourselves, and ordered pastries and tea. Elizabeth sighed audibly and looked about as she removed her right glove.

"This is a lovely room, don't you think?" she asked.

"Yes, it is nice. The silk wall coverings and chandeliers are quite tasteful. Not the gaudy things you see in some of the seedier establishments," I responded.

"And you've been in these seedy establishments?" she teased.

"Yes, actually."

"What on earth were you doing there?" Elizabeth asked, showing that the notion disconcerted her.

"It was during the war. One of the hotels in Norwich had

been converted to a hospital. We spent weeks scrubbing walls and floors, and they still looked awful." I shuddered at the memory of the faded wallpaper and leaky lamps. "Oh, do not look so appalled. I was a member of a soldier aid society that worked with the Sanitary. I sewed hospital shirts, knitted socks, and rolled bandages and delivered them to the hospital."

"Yes, I did similar work but never visited the hospitals." Elizabeth stared into the past.

The pastries and tea were placed on the table. I poured while Elizabeth selected a pastry. There were few people in the dining room at that hour, allowing us a clear view of the entry.

I looked up as I set down the teapot and gasped. My friend looked up and uttered, "Great heavenly days." I could not think. We could not leave the restaurant without calling attention to ourselves. I wished I had worn a veil to cover my face.

We were frozen to our chairs, the tea and pastries forgotten.

Josiah Pennyman had seen us and walked, purposely, toward our table.

"Just what the hell do you think you're doing here, Miss Llewellyn?" Josiah asked as he arrived at our table.

"I am enjoying a pleasant morning with my friend." I hoped my voice sounded casual, not betraying the fear I felt. "How is it that you are back from New Mexico so soon?"

"Jake Tolliver rode out and found me. He told a tale about you and all my house servants being involved in some kind of donnybrook. I feared for your safety and thought I best come back." He spoke quietly so that only Elizabeth and I could hear him.

Without invitation, he looked about, took a chair from

another table, and seated himself backward on the chair across from me. "You two can come on home with me."

"I am sorry, Mr. Pennyman, but I did leave a letter giving notice. I shall not be returning to Gehenna," Elizabeth looked him full in the face and spoke in a level voice.

"Where are Mrs. Hudson and Mrs. O'Malley?" he asked.

"Gone. They left the city two weeks hence," I informed him. "I shall not be going with you, either. Whatever business arrangements you made with my father, neither of you had the right to use me as payment of a debt. The thirteenth amendment has been ratified. Slavery and involuntary servitude are no longer lawful, or did you miss that announcement, Mr. Pennyman?" I was warming to my task, aware that it would be dangerous to push him too far.

"I do wonder what Dear Father told you. I shall not deny our partnership did not end well. Angry words were spoken on both sides. But, be clear about this: Our betrothal has nothing to do with any business I had with your father. Come, my dearest, we'll ask the reverend to marry us before we return to the ranch."

"Your mind seems to be addled. Perhaps you spent too many hours in the sun with your cattle. My recollection is that you broke the engagement and forced me into servitude. No, Mr. Josiah Pennyman, I shall not become your wife. Nor shall I return to your ranch and your half-finished house. I shall leave this godforsaken state. And, when I do, I shall never think of you or this place ever again."

Josiah was taken aback by this speech. "I declare, you do have an imagination. My temper ran loose before I left for New Mexico. I am sorry for that. Let's agree to call it a lover's spat and restart our lives together."

I was incredulous. "I would rather rot in Hell than go anywhere with you. Now, if you will excuse us, I have quite lost my appetite, and we must finish our errands." Elizabeth and I rose, gathered our parcels, and prepared to leave.

"I'm afraid I cannot allow that, Priscilla. You are my betrothed. Your father wanted us to build a life together, to give him grandchildren. You wouldn't want to disappoint your dear father, would you?" Josiah's voice was still calm but had a certain edge, warning me that his patience was running short.

"And, just how do you know what my father wants? He's halfway round the globe," I challenged. "Now, you will allow us to pass. Good day, Mr. Pennyman."

"As you wish, my dear. But know that this is not finished. I shall have you back."

I ignored the comment, paid the bill, and left the hotel, hoping he would not follow us.

Out on the street, Elizabeth and I looked at each other, fright reflected in her eyes.

"What are we to do now?" she asked.

"We shall go to Sheriff Berry and inform him that Josiah is in town," I replied, shaken but retaining control over my faculties. We headed toward the sheriff's office, hoping against hope that he would be there.

Sheriff Henry Berry was walking across the street toward his office as we approached from the opposite direction.

"Miss Llewellyn, Mrs. Owens, to what do I owe this pleasure?" he asked as he stepped up onto the wooden walkway and tipped his hat.

"I am afraid this is not a social call, Sheriff," I said. "We just engaged in a most unpleasant conversation with Josiah

Pennyman. He has decided that I ought to marry him and accompany him to Gehenna."

Astonishment registered on his face for just a moment before he recovered himself. "Well, that is an interesting turn of events, isn't it." He looked thoughtful. "Where are my manners? Ladies, do come inside." The sheriff opened the door and stood aside for us to pass.

Once we were settled in chairs in front of his desk, he looked at each of us. "Mrs. Owens, does he wish you to return, too?"

"He did say so, but I pointed out that I left a letter giving notice, and he then ignored me. He also asked after Mrs. Hudson and Mrs. O'Malley. We told him they had left the city, but not where they went."

"Josiah claims that he was not himself when he mistreated me," I added. "He prevaricates, Sheriff, and will stop at nothing to get what he wants. I believe my life to be in great danger.

"We have booked passage on the *Lorena*. I want nothing more than to be on board that ship tomorrow morning. Please, you must help us."

The lawman leaned back in his chair and looked at the ceiling of the small office. He remained in this posture for quite some time, and I feared he might fall asleep. Finally, he sat upright, the front legs of his chair thumping on the wooden floor. He leapt to his feet, snatched his hat from the rack, looked over his shoulder, and said, "Come with me, ladies."

We looked at each other, questions on our faces, but gathered our parcels and began to follow him.

"Leave those packages on the desk. I'll have my deputy deliver them to the boardinghouse." He waved his hand vaguely in the direction from which he had just come. Then he shouted, "Boone, you back there?"

A slight, almost frail young man shambled out from the back of the building. "Ain't no call to bellow, Henry. I kin hear jes fine."

"Boone, take those parcels to Mrs. Dolan's. Tell her not to fret about these ladies. They are well but won't be back till late tonight."

Without a moment's hesitation, Boone moved slowly toward the desk to do as he was told. We followed the sheriff outside and away from the shopping district.

The sheriff walked quickly, taking us on a tour of the seamier parts of Corpus Christi. We kept near him, grateful our wide skirts allowed for long strides. He slowed his pace, looking carefully at houses on a street where six filthy, poorly dressed children played in the mud at the base of a water pump.

He looked at one house, set slightly back from the others on the street. Turning toward the children, he called, "Is your mama in the house?"

A young girl in a tattered pink dress stood up, watching the man with suspicion. "Is Papa gettin' outta jail?"

"No, Carolyn." He spoke softly, his face contorted in a way I did not understand. "He's goin' to be gone a long time. I just need to talk to your mama. These ladies need her help."

"She went down to the church to talk to Reverend Phillips. She said she had to ask him a real important question."

"How long ago did she go down there?"

"I don't know. Maggie was just up from her nap, and Mama said I was to watch her while she went out. Papa don't know Mama talks to Reverend Phillips. It's a secret."

"We'll keep her secret. We just need to talk with her.

We'll wait up on the porch."

"Papa don't like people comin' onto our property."

"Don't you worry none about your Papa. Go on and play with your brothers and sisters." He turned toward the house, beckoning Elizabeth and me to follow him.

Elizabeth took a step nearer the children, a peculiar expression on her face. "Carolyn? Carolyn Campbell?" she called.

"Elizabeth," the child exclaimed, running to the former maid.

Two of the children looked up from their mud pies and abandoned them to come to greet Elizabeth.

Sheriff Berry stopped and turned to observe the scene. "You know these children?" he asked, incredulity in his voice.

"Yes, I was their nanny during our trip from California to Texas." Elizabeth was failing in her attempts to avoid the embraces the children wanted to bestow upon her. Mud speckled the skirt of her dress.

"This changes everything," the lawman mused.

"Why?" I asked but received no reply.

"Children, Mrs. Owens must leave now. Say goodbye." Turning toward me, the sheriff continued, "Their mother won't want to see Mrs. Owens."

"And why would that be?" I asked cautiously.

"Ian Campbell was killed in a gunfight in his saloon over a year ago. His widow, Miranda, married Patrick Higgins about three months later. Said she had no time for mourning what with the young 'uns," the lawman explained.

"You mean to tell us that Elizabeth traveled from California with Patrick Higgins' widow?" It was my turn to be incredulous.

"Well, Miss, it might not have been my best plan, but it's what came to mind. She's got all these little ones to feed and no income to speak of." He seemed regretful of the circumstances.

"I don't believe Mrs. Camp...Higgins will be disposed to lift a finger to help me," Elizabeth observed. "She must know what happened." My friend dug into her reticule, pulled out her handkerchief, and commenced to dab at her eyes.

Turning our backs on the children, we began following the sheriff down the track. We hadn't gotten far when we saw a comely woman making her way toward us. She was dressed quite fashionably, not at all suited for this neighborhood. She was not looking ahead but kept her eyes downcast.

As we drew closer to the woman, Elizabeth paled and gasped, "Oh my."

"Are you ill?" I put a hand on her elbow to help steady her.

"I am well. She has changed considerably since I last laid eyes on her."

When we were within speaking distance, the sheriff said, "We don't want no trouble, Matilda."

The woman looked up, seemingly surprised to see anyone on the road. Recognizing Elizabeth, she turned to look at the sheriff. "What do you mean bringing that woman here? Is she the one what kilt my Patrick?" She stood a little taller and trained a venomous glare on Elizabeth.

"I made a mistake. I thought I could help you and these ladies simultaneously," the lawman explained.

"Help me? How? By bringing my husband's murderess to my home?" Matilda Higgins' face was crimson, and the volume of her voice was rising. "This woman near ruined my children with all her talk of book-learning. They'd rather go to school than work to put food on our table." She spat on the street. "Fat lot of good reading and arithmetic will do them now they have no father." The bitterness in her voice would have been moving had the expression on her face matched the sentiment.

"Calm down, Matilda," the sheriff said. "There's no reason to get all riled up. We'll be on our way." Having taken less than ten steps, the sheriff stopped and twisted his body to face the woman and her children. "Josiah Pennyman is in need of a cook. He's staying at the Union House." He turned and continued walking.

Our next stop was a little church. It was brilliant white, as though it had been newly painted. A man, in the manner of dress that identified him as a minister, was crawling about the lawn, stopping occasionally to pull a weed and place it in a potato sack.

"Reverend Phillips?" the sheriff called as we approached the man.

The vicar looked up. Seeing us coming, he stood, wiping the soil from his hands. Leaves and blades of grass clung to the knees of his trousers.

"What brings you out this way on such a fine day?" the minister asked.

"I had a harebrained idea that went sour. These ladies require a place to stay out of the main until after dark," the sheriff explained.

"I see." The reverend's reply was terse. "And, of course, you thought to bring them here to seek sanctuary."

"Well, yes. You being a good Christian man, I assumed you could help out a couple of damsels in distress."

I was having difficulty believing the behavior of both men. They seemed to be at odds, but an undertone to the sheriff's speech led me to believe this banter was nothing more than a game to them.

“Why not? I have nothing better to do with my evening. My social calendar seems to be quite empty tonight.” Reverend Phillps turned and started walking toward the side of the church. He looked over his shoulder toward us. “Come along with me to the parsonage.”

We hurried to keep up with the minister. He led us into a small, neat cottage adjacent to the church.

After seeing us settled in the parlor and introductions made, the minister went to the door and shouted, “Mrs. Henderson, we have guests.” He then settled himself in a worn wing chair next to the fireplace. “What brings you out this way, Henry?”

“These ladies are in need of a place to stay out of sight until after dark. Miss Llewellyn’s life may depend upon it,” the sheriff explained.

“Aren’t you being a tad melodramatic?” the clergyman asked.

“Not at all, Luke. The man lookin’ for her is dangerous as they come. He’ll stop at nothing to get her.”

“So, Josiah Pennyman is back, is he.” It was more of a statement than a question. “Well, then, the ladies are welcome to stay here, but Mrs. Henderson does not live in.” He thought a few minutes. “Does Mrs. Higgins know he’s back?”

“Well, yes. I told her where to find him. Thought he might be disposed to hire her on as his cook, bein’ as he’s the reason she’s now a widow.”

The Reverend Luke Phillips groaned loudly and sunk his head between his hands. “Oh, Henry, what have you done?”

The sheriff looked puzzled. Dread spread across his countenance. “Damn my eyes. I just led Pennyman here.”

Our vulnerability was not lost on either Elizabeth or me. My right hand instinctively found her left and squeezed so tightly that I heard her gasp.

Mrs. Henderson selected this moment to come in, plates, flatware, and glassware rattling on the tray she carried. Quietly and efficiently, she poured lemonade, delivered glasses, and offered cakes and cookies to each of us. Satisfied she had done her duty, she glanced at the mantel clock, dropped a curtsy, and left, closing the door.

Elizabeth broke the silence, asking, "Does Mrs. Felton still run her boardinghouse on High Street?"

"Yes, she does," Sheriff Berry answered. "Why do you ask?"

"I was one of her boarders when I first arrived in Corpus Christi. I do not believe she is acquainted with either Mr. Pennyman or Mrs. Higgins. She may be willing to help us," the former maid explained.

After brief consideration, Sheriff Berry remarked, "She could well be willing. I'll go see her." He stood to leave.

"I shall accompany you, Henry. Give me a moment to ask Mrs. Henderson to stay with the ladies while we're gone." Reverend Phillips seemed quite excited.

"No, Luke, you need to stay here," Henry Berry admonished.

"If you're worried about protecting the ladies, Mrs. Henderson is better with a shotgun than I ever will be." The minister said, a bit shamefaced.

"All right, let's get going before I change my mind," the older man agreed.

The reverend went to the door and called to his housekeeper. Mrs. Henderson agreed to stay until his return.

The mantel clock chimed the hour twice before the men returned in a delivery van. We had little time to thank

Reverend Phillips and Mrs. Henderson before we were bustled into the conveyance and whisked off to High Street.

Sheriff Berry drove around to the back of Mrs. Felton's house and assisted our disembarking. Mrs. Felton came out to greet us and invited us inside. We entered the house through a lovely kitchen, enveloped with the wonderful fragrance of baking bread.

"Let's go through to the parlor, where it is cooler." Mrs. Felton held the door for us to pass into a hallway leading to the sitting room.

"Thank you for helping us," Elizabeth said. "I am so sorry I haven't been to visit before now."

"I quite understand. I saw the articles in the newspaper and recognized your name. I am relieved with the outcome," the landlady said. "Please, make yourselves comfortable. Supper will be served early this evening. Several of my boarders have plans to attend an entertainment."

"I'll be back to fetch you ladies around 9:30," the sheriff said.

"They will be safe here. I'll see that they come to no harm," Mrs. Felton assured him.

The sheriff left the way he came.

Mrs. Felton, Elizabeth, and I agreed it would be best that her boarders not know we were in the house. The landlady led us to a small sitting room off the kitchen.

The room was well-appointed with stuffed furniture. The floral pattern of the chintz slipcovers and curtains gave an air of femininity to the space. The wood tables and chairs gleamed with recently applied wax. The crystal drops encircling china lamps cast rainbows on the walls. Miniatures of unnamed persons were hung above a chest of drawers. A rustic wood cross hung over a desk, where a Bible lay open, as though someone's devotions had been interrupted. Removing our hats and gloves, we made ourselves comfortable while waiting for the sun to set.

Theodora Felton proved herself a hospitable woman, concerned with our comfort and nourishment. Elizabeth and I whiled away the afternoon playing Piquet with cards lent us by our hostess.

With such pleasant diversions, the darkness came upon us quickly. Mrs. Felton came and lit the lamps and closed the curtains tightly to ensure no light would sneak out into the night.

Sheriff Berry appeared at the kitchen door at the appointed time. Elizabeth and I thanked Mrs. Felton profusely for granting us sanctuary. Donning our bonnets and gloves, we followed our guide into the night.

Staying close to the sheriff, we quickly moved from shadow to shadow, keeping near buildings. We were soon walking down the center of Chaparral Street, doing our best to stay out of the light of the lanterns hung on the outer walls, as well as the light spilling from the windows and open doors of the drinking establishments.

I thought us safe as we passed through town and toward neat rows of houses and our destination. Having kept my eyes fixed on Sheriff Berry's back, I heard, rather than saw, someone step onto the sandy street, bits of dirt and stones crunching underfoot.

The three of us stopped and listened. An owl hooted. A dog barked. The crickets sang their love songs. These sounds of the night were heard over our labored breathing. We took a few cautious steps. The out-of-cadence footfalls resumed as well.

The lawman motioned us to move next to the wall of a

nearby house with dark windows. We tried very hard to place our feet as quietly as possible, but the coarse soil and small pebbles would not be silent.

The three of us hugged the wall. I trembled in fear of who was following us.

The sheriff called out, "Who goes there? Show yerself."

Only the sounds of the night. Someone inside the house began snoring, startling me. I tried to stifle the "Oh" that escaped. Elizabeth squeezed my arm. I found her hand and gripped it tightly.

"I know you're out there," Sheriff Berry persisted. "Identify yerself."

Snoring and crickets.

A tug on my sleeve signaled me to continue our trek. We were but a few streets from Mrs. Dolan's boardinghouse, and safety.

I was directly behind the lawman, with Elizabeth bringing up the end of our little parade. We walked quickly, the out-of-step crunching noise roaring in my ears.

A piercing scream echoed through the night. I stood stalk still, but the sheriff seized my wrist and pulled me along to the first house we came upon with lamps illuminating the windows. He pounded the door with his fist, calling out, "This is Sheriff Berry. Open up."

The door was cracked open, a single eye visible below a lacy nightcap. "What do you mean frightening an old lady out of her last years?" a frail voice asked.

"I beg pardon, Mrs. Kennedy. Please, shelter this lady while I deal with a rascal." The lawman put his hand on my back and pushed. I stumbled through the door. The old woman squealed and fell backward into a wall. Unable to stop my forward momentum, the lady and I collided, landing on the floor in a heap of muslin and silk. The door slammed shut behind us as Mrs. Kennedy and I gained our feet and composure.

"Who are you?" the old woman asked in an accusatory tone.

"My name is Priscilla Llewellyn. I am pleased to make your acquaintance, though I am sorry for the circumstances," I said, settling my underskirts and smoothing out my dress.

"Who's chasing you?"

"A dreadful man." I did not intend to be cryptic but saw no reason to further involve the lady in my plight.

"Well, there's more than one of those in this city. You best come in and sit while you wait for Henry to come for you."

She had no sooner stopped speaking than there was a sharp rap on the door. We looked at each other and back at the door.

"Mrs. Kennedy. It's Henry Berry. Open the door."

The lady obeyed. I was relieved to see Elizabeth standing behind him.

"Well, come on in. I'd no idea I was to entertain in my nightdress, but there you are." Mrs. Kennedy held the door wide while the two remained outside.

"I am sorry for the intrusion, Mrs. Kennedy. But these ladies have had a time of it of late. We won't trouble you further. Good night to you," the sheriff said, looking kindly at the woman and beckoning me to follow him.

Out in the street, we once again kept to the shadows. There was no time to ask what had happened to Elizabeth. That story would have to keep.

We wound our way through the streets, past houses, for what seemed to be hours. I had long since given up any attempt to ascertain where we were. About the time I despaired of ever seeing Mrs. Dolan's house, we turned a corner, and there it was.

A light could be seen burning in the drawing room and one of the upstairs bedrooms. There was no movement outside save our own. Still, we kept to the shadows, creeping along the neat, whitewashed picket fences that bordered the yards of the adjacent houses.

Stopping at the corner of the boardinghouse, the lawman motioned to us to sit where we were and keep quiet. Elizabeth and I complied, the skirts of our dresses collapsing in circles around each of us.

Crouching down to make himself as small as possible, the sheriff moved through the shadows cautiously toward our destination, looking about him as he went.

"I knew you had to return, eventually." Josiah Pennyman's voice was nearly a whisper.

I grasped Elizabeth's hand but did not speak.

"Come now. You ought not to be skulking about in the night like a thief."

I remained mute and clung to Elizabeth.

"Why do you persist in evading me? I mean you no harm. Just stop all this foolishness and return to the hotel with me."

I could see his hand held out toward me in the moonlight. Neither Elizabeth nor I moved but sat with our backs against the fence, praying the sheriff would return for us soon.

"Priscilla, get up," Josiah ordered, impatience tingeing his words.

I shivered, though the night was warm, but made no motion to comply with the command.

He kicked a dirt clod down the street in frustration but kept his voice low. "If you don't rise of your own volition, I shall carry you off."

I had no time to react. Hands were laid upon me, lifting me off the ground and wresting me away from Elizabeth's grasp.

A scream pierced the night, though I have no memory of opening my mouth. Josiah roughly threw me over his shoulder in the manner he would handle a large sack of flour, turned, and started to walk away.

I lifted my head but could see neither Elizabeth nor the sheriff in the inky night. I pummeled Josiah's back with my fists and shouted, "Help! Help me." I wriggled, trying to dislodge his arm clamped tightly around my lower limbs.

"Stop where you are, Pennyman, and set the woman on her feet," a disembodied voice said. I heard the distinctive click-click-click of a revolver being cocked.

"Get out of our way, Sheriff. I aim to take her to wife." Josiah increased the pressure on my lower limbs.

The sheriff huffed. "Miss Llewellyn, do you desire to wed this man?" he asked.

"Definitely not," I responded.

"You heard the lady. Set her feet on the ground and walk away before there is more trouble." Henry Berry ordered.

"Her father made a bargain, and she is mine," Josiah persisted. "Step aside, Sheriff, and let us pass."

"I ain't gonna do that, Pennyman."

"Then it seems we have a stalemate," Pennyman said.

A cloud passed from in front of the moon, and I saw Elizabeth slowly rise to stand where we had been sitting, her back still toward the fence.

I stopped struggling and hoped my voice would convey a calmness I did not feel. "Josiah put me down. Nothing good will come from carrying me off like this."

"No, I don't think I shall," he replied. "Sheriff, I'm taking her, like it or not."

"Mrs. Owens, kindly remove yourself from behind these two. Go on to the boardinghouse. There ain't no reason for you to be involved in this," the lawman called out. "Pennyman, I'll tell you one last time—let the lady go."

Josiah shifted his grip on me. I once again heard that distinctive clicking sound. I was jolted by the recoil of his body as the pistol discharged into the ground. "Let us pass, Sheriff, and no blood will be spilled tonight."

The sounds of feet shifting on dirt alerted me. I lifted my head to see several townsmen come into the open. James Kilpatrick and Lieutenant Grayson were there, as well as others I did not know. The lieutenant held a sword in his left hand, the point angled slightly to the ground. His right hand held his revolver.

Josiah slowly turned around, allowing me to see that we were surrounded by men with all manner of firearms.

"Let me go, Josiah. You don't want me for your wife any more than I wish to wed you," I pled.

"Your loving parent is a cheat and a liar. He never sent the gold he promised. He probably took it with him. So, I'll keep you."

Frightened and weary of the entire affair, I hung limply over Josiah's shoulder, unwilling to make any attempt to speak.

No one spoke or moved. I prayed that none of the townsmen would shoot indiscriminately.

Josiah turned in a circle. A dog barked, and another answered.

"Pennyman, you have to the count of three to set Miss Llewellyn on her feet," Sheriff Berry announced.

"Make a hole. Let us pass," Josiah retorted.

"One..."

Josiah took a step forward.

"Two..."

Another step. The men in the circle behind Josiah faded into the darkness.

"Three."

I saw a flash moments before I heard the report of a rifle being fired. Josiah staggered but kept on his feet and retained his hold on me. His pistol slipped from his hand and landed in the dirt with a thud.

He sank slowly to the ground, loosening his grip, and I rolled away from him onto the dirt road.

Several men rushed to assist me in gaining my feet. I tried to turn to look at my captor, but strong arms kept me turned away and guided me toward Mrs. Dolan's house.

Elizabeth opened the door as I was escorted up the walk. She hugged me and led me into the drawing room.

Once installed in a chair, I was plied with strong hot tea liberally laced with brandy. I felt curiously calm and absently wondered how seriously Josiah had been injured.

The room was crowded with people, all watching me and waiting expectantly for someone to tell them what had just transpired. I was in a daze, seeing these people as though in a dream.

"Would you all please go outside or into the dining room? Give Miss Llewellyn some air," a masculine voice pierced through the veil of fog surrounding me.

As people filed out of the room, Mrs. Dolan protectively hovered over Elizabeth and me.

When most everyone was gone, Mrs. Dolan went to the kitchen to refresh the teapot. Quietude descended upon the room, to be broken by the sound of shoes on wood floors. James Kilpatrick and Lieutenant Grayson stood before us.

“I know you’re upset, Miss Llewellyn, but I must ask you a few questions,” the lieutenant said.

“Can’t it wait for her to catch her breath?” Elizabeth asked.

“I wish it could, but no. We need to know now.” There was a note of regret in the young officer’s voice.

“It’s all right.” I heard myself say. Looking down at my blood-splattered dress, I absently wondered where the bright red stains came from but heard the rifle report in my head and shuddered.

“Are you injured?” James asked, kneeling in front of me.

Somewhat detached from the scene, I looked up at the man I’d known in Connecticut and wondered when he had come in.

“No,” I responded in a small voice. “Is he...”

“He’s still breathing. No telling how long he’ll draw it out.”

I did not understand what he was telling me. “Draw out what?”

“They don’t expect Pennyman will recover from his injury.”

“Oh, I see. Where was he...”

“Don’t you worry yourself about that, Priscilla. We thought we should check on you.”

“I should have stayed in New Orleans,” I said.

“I beg your pardon, Miss?” the lieutenant asked.

“She’s not herself. She needs time and rest. Can’t you gentlemen talk with her tomorrow?” Mrs. Dolan asked.

“No,” I said, the haze in my head lifting a little. “I’m going to Indianola tomorrow. I have to talk with these men now.” I looked down at my dress again and started to stand. “Look at this dress. I can’t be receiving callers in a soiled dress. I must go change it now.” I left the drawing room and went upstairs to make myself presentable.

I returned a few minutes later, having washed my face and changed into a clean dress. More determined than ever to be on the *Lorena* in the morning, I forced myself out of the malaise I had fallen into and was prepared to answer any questions the lieutenant might pose.

Upon entering the drawing room, I was surprised to find Sheriff Berry sitting in the overstuffed chair, a glass of spirits in his hand.

"I just wanted to assure you ladies that you're free to leave Corpus Christi tomorrow. There ain't no reason for either of you to give witness to anything that happened tonight. If the judge won't believe me, he ain't likely to believe anyone," the lawman said. He downed his drink in one swallow, stood, and placed the tumbler on the side table. "I got a long night ahead of me. Good night, and good luck to you both." He left the room and walked out the front door, his head hanging low and his hat still in his hand.

Long after all the visitors had left and Mrs. Dolan sought her bed, Elizabeth and I sat alone in the drawing room. Quietly, I asked, "What happened to you?"

"When?" she countered.

"Just before the sheriff pushed me into Mrs. Kennedy's house."

"Mr. Pennyman nabbed me and carried me some distance in a most unseemly posture. He thought I was you. As soon as he realized his error, he released me and faded into the night. I was making my way back here when Sheriff Berry found me, and we went to Mrs. Kennedy's."

I felt compelled to apologize again for involving her in my problems, but I kept silent and sipped my tea. A rap on the door interrupted our reverie. I was only vaguely aware of Elizabeth going to see who was at the door at this ghastly hour.

She returned, followed by James. "I beg pardon for the intrusion, but I saw the light and thought you would want to know."

"Know what?" Elizabeth and I asked.

"Pennyman's dead. He passed about twenty minutes ago."

It is always an unhappy moment when a soul leaves this earth. After all, that person, however hateful, was someone's son, brother, father, friend. But I felt only relief in hearing the news of Josiah's passing. Perhaps now, I would be able to put my life in order without fear.

"Thank you for coming," I said, standing to come to him.

"I'll let myself out. I just wanted to pass on the news." He turned and left quietly.

When we heard the door shut, we extinguished the lamps and went to bed.

Chapter 20

Elizabeth and I were to board the ship no later than nine o'clock, with the ship actually getting under sail sometime after ten. Mr. Mitchell and Robert had carried our trunks downstairs to the foyer before breakfast.

James arrived just before eight o'clock that morning. Banjo, looking quite himself again, was pulling a hired wagon. The Mitchells and Mr. Kilpatrick loaded the luggage. He gave the hardware store proprietor a ride to his shop on the way to the wharf to deposit our baggage with the ship steward.

Elizabeth and I said our goodbyes to Mrs. Dolan and Samantha. We hugged our landlady, thanking her for accepting us as boarders through tearful goodbyes.

At half-past eight, he returned, handed us up onto the seat of the wagon, settled himself next to me, and took the reins in hand. Banjo wended his way through the city to the wharf with confidence, as though he did it every day of his life.

After we were assisted down from the wagon, Elizabeth, James, and I walked onto the dock where a lighter was moored. He spoke with the pilot and said a perfunctory farewell to Elizabeth. As she was being assisted onto the barge, the attorney turned to me and took my left hand in his.

"I shall never be able to thank you for everything you have done for me," I said, gripping his fingers tightly and choking back tears. "I am so sorry for the trouble I have caused you."

"It has been no trouble. In fact, it has been my pleasure to be of assistance to you, Priscilla. Do write when you are settled. Just to let me know you are well."

"I shall, though I suspect it may be some months."

"The pilot looks anxious to get underway. Goodbye, Priscilla. Safe travels." He lowered his voice to a whisper. "I shall miss you."

"Thank you."

He raised my left hand, kissing it lightly as he bowed. I did not try to stop the tears that spilled onto my cheeks as he led me to the waiting boat.

The pilot took my hand and assisted me aboard. I waved to James Kilpatrick and watched the wharf grow smaller as the lighter moved away from the dock toward the channels leading to the open sea, the *Lorena,* and a new life.

The End

THANK YOU

Thank you for taking the time to read *Priscilla Alone*. I hope you enjoyed Priscilla's story.

If so inclined, please leave a review with Amazon or Goodreads.

Look for *Together Alone*—Book 2 of The Alone Trilogy.

ACKNOWLEDGMENTS

I relied upon *The Story of Corpus Christi* by Mrs. Mary A. Sutherland, published in 1916 by the Corpus Christi Chapter of Daughters of the Confederacy, for information relating to daily life in Corpus Christi, Texas, during the spring of 1866. I also referred to *Historical Review of Southeast Texas and the Founders, Leaders, and Representative Men of its Commerce, Industry, and Civic Affairs, Volume 2* Edited by Dermot H Hardy, B.A. and Major Ingham S. Roberts, published by the Lewis Publishing Company in 1910.

But for the support of the Visalia and Exeter Writers' Groups, this novel may have languished in my computer forever. Jay Johnson and his living history impression of a Civil War-era Confederate blockade runner gave me invaluable information regarding shipping during the mid-nineteenth century.

I am eternally grateful to my beta readers and to Victoria for collaborating with me on the cover.

Lastly, a heartfelt thank you to my husband. He was, and continues to be, a sounding board and a great source of trivia.

ABOUT THE AUTHOR

Judith Bixby-Boling has been reading and writing most of her life. She utilizes her research and writing skills honed while working as a paralegal and then as a construction specifier.

Boling and her husband are members of an American Civil War reenacting group. Her interest in this era is reflected in her writing.

She lives with her husband in Central California.

FOR MORE INFORMATION ABOUT JUDITH BIXBY-BOLING VISIT:

judithbixbyboling.net

FOLLOW HER ON:

Facebook
Instagram
LinkedIn
X

www.ingramcontent.com/pod-product-compliance
Lightning Source LLC
LaVergne TN
LVHW091128080826
845145LV00008B/2085